THE SPACE ADVENTURE NOVELS
OF
ANDRE NORTON

SARGASSO OF SPACE
PLAGUE SHIP
VOODOO PLANET and STAR HUNTER
THE CROSSROADS OF TIME
SECRET OF THE LOST RACE
THE SIOUX SPACEMAN

THE
CROSSROADS
OF
TIME

BY

ANDRE NORTON

GREGG PRESS
BOSTON

THE CROSSROADS OF TIME

This edition published in 1978 by Gregg Press
A Division of G. K. Hall & Co.
by arrangement with Ace Books, Inc.
and with the cooperation of Andre Norton

Jacket art by Jack Gaughan
Title Page art and design by Elizabeth R. Cooke

Printed on permanent/durable acid-free paper and bound
in the United States of America

First Printing, February 1978

Library of Congress Cataloging in Publication Data

Norton, Andre.
The crossroads of time.

(The space adventure novels of Andre Norton)
Reprint of the ed. published by Ace Books, New York
I. Title. II. Series: Norton, Andre. The space
adventure novels of Andre Norton.
PZ3.N8187Cp   1978   [PS3527.0625]   813'.5'2   77-25531
ISBN 0-8398-2418-1

PROLOGUE

THE OFFICE was bare of all furniture except for a seat pulled drawer fashion out of the softly glowing wall. The report shining in fiery script up at the Inspector was on a desk. Or perhaps those letters only appeared fiery because of the possible conflagration to come, masked in the official idiom of his particular security section. As long ago as his third month in the Service, a time now he found difficult to recall, he had ceased abruptly to believe that any operation could run smoothly. In past experience the most placid landscapes hid the nastiest traps.

Now he leaned back in the seat which accommodatingly changed shape to fit his middle-aged bulk at the new angle. Though his expression had not changed, he ran a finger tip nervously back and forth along the edge of the reader plate on which the message still stood. He had already wasted too much time on this, but—

CLASSIFIED REPORT: Division 1 Plus Information
PROJECT: 4678
NATURE OF OFFENSE: Attempt to influence other
level history.

AGENTS:
      Section Leader: Com Varlt, MW 69321
      Crew: Horman Tilis MW 69345
                    Fal Korf AW 70958
                    Pague Lo Sig AW 70889

PROGRESS TO DATE:
Traced subject—Kmoat Vo Pranj—to Levels 415-426 inclusive. Established prime base on likeliest world (E641—marked, on survey of Kol 30, 51446 E. C. as "culturally retarded, critical, forbidden, except to sociological investigators, rank I-2"). But subject may be on another world of this grouping or engaged in hopping.

COVER:

Have assumed credentials and background of members of native law enforcement body, national in scope (Federal Bureau of Investigation).

TYPE OF CULTURE:

Dawn atomic—inhabitants on this level appear to possess no psi powers—highly unstable civilization —just the type to attract Pranj.

REMARKS:

There was the meat of it, entered under "remarks." The Inspector's eyes lifted to the restful, unbroken glow of the opposite wall. They were getting all too many of such "remarks" at Headquarters lately. Why, when he had been in the field force—He shook his head and then had the grace to laugh at his own dawning pomposity. The important point was—the man in the field *knew*. He read the final sentence on which his decision must be made.

REMARKS:

Must term operation "solution dubious"—critical plus—require extreme powers under 202 classification.

Com Varlt, MW in charge.

Com Varlt. The Inspector triggered a button with one of those nervous finger tips. The report flashed off and in its place was a series of code symbols. Hmm, that agent had a rather impressive record all the way along. The Inspector's hesitation was gone. He pressed a second button and smiled almost grimly. Varlt had asked for it —now he had his wish. Only "solution dubious" had better turn out "Solution Satisfactory"! A new report clicked on the reader and the Inspector turned to consider another case.

CHAPTER ONE

THE WINDOW was a square of gray light at the narrow end
of the small hotel room. Blake Walker regarded this evidence of another day with an odd detachment. He
moved—to snub out a cigarette in the tray beside the
bed. Then he collected his watch from the table. A minute past six. And what he had been waiting for the past
hour must be very close now—

He pulled his six feet of lean muscle and fine bones out
of the bed and padded into the bathroom to plug in his
razor. From the mirror his own eyes, tired and dark,
stared back at him without curiosity or interest. In the
artificial light his thick cap of hair appeared as black as
his brows and lashes—but in the sun light it would be
red, so dark a red as might rightly be termed mahogany.
Only his skin was not fair, but a smooth and even brown,
as if before birth he had acquired a permanent sun tan.

Shaving was a perfunctory business, conducted mostly
from force of habit, since his area of beard was small and
grew slowly. His black brows twisted together now in a
familiar frown as he wondered, for perhaps the thou-
sandth time, if he did have Asiatic blood. Only, who had
ever heard of a red-haired Chinese or Hindu? Not that he
could trace his parentage. Detective Sergeant Dan
Walker had brought the resources of an entire city police
force to bear on that problem some twenty years ago,
after he had stumbled on the "alley baby." Patrolman
Harvey Blake and Sergeant Dan Walker had found him
and later Dan had claimed him for a son. But he would

7

always wonder about the two years of his life before that.

Blake's well-cut mouth became a grim line under the pressure of memory. Sergeant—now Inspector—Dan going into the First National to buy traveler's checks for that long-awaited trip—running into a holdup in progress. Dan Walker had been shot down and it had not lessened Molly's heartache to know that he had taken his killer with him. After that there had been the two of them, Molly Walker and Blake. Then Molly went to bed one night and did not awake in the morning.

So now he was alone again, cut off from the only security he had known. Blake put down the razor carefully as if that motion was a part of some intricate and necessary action. His eyes were still on the mirror, but they saw no reflection there, certainly not the lines of tension suddenly aging his face. It was coming—it was very close now!

The last time that feeling had driven him into Molly's bedroom and his painful discovery there. Now it was urgently pushing him toward the hall. He listened, knowing of old that there was really nothing to hear—this he could only feel. Then, with quiet cat's feet, he went to the hall door without snapping on the room light.

With infinite caution he turned the key and eased the door open. He had no idea of what waited on the other side—he only knew that some action was being so forceably demanded of him that he could not disobey even if he wished.

For one moment he stared. Two men stood, their backs toward him, one behind the other. A tall man wearing a loose coat, his dark hair still glistening with the sheen of sleet, was fitting a key into the door on the opposite side of the corridor. His companion held a gun jammed against his back.

Blake, his bare feet making no sound on the carpet,

moved. His fingers locked about the gunman's throat and he jerked the fellow's head back. Instantly the other man whirled. Almost, Blake thought, as if he had known what was about to happen. His fist swung up and connected with just the right point on the threshing captive's jaw; then Blake was supporting the full weight of an unconscious man. But the other took hold, waving Blake back into his room, following him quickly, the prize in tow. Once inside he dropped his burden to the floor without ceremony and locked the door.

With a doubt or two, Blake sat down on the edge of the bed. Why so little fuss on the part of the suddenly released prisoner? And why come in here with the captive?

"Police———?" His hand went to the phone on the bedside table.

The tall man turned. He brought out a wallet and flipped it open for Blake to read the card inside. Then the younger man nodded.

"No police?"

The other shook his head. "Not yet. Sorry to barge in on you, Mr.—Mr.?"

"Walker."

"Mr. Walker. You helped me out of a tight hole there. But I'll have to ask you to let me handle this my own way. We won't bother you for long."

"I'll finish dressing," Blake got up.

The Federal Agent was squatting on his heels by the slumbering gunman. And Blake was knotting his tie when a scene, reflected in the mirror, drew him back to the bedroom. The self-introduced Kittson was searching his unconscious prisoner and the oddness of that search intrigued Blake.

Slowly the Federal man ran his fingers through the oily hair of the other, apparently in quest of something on the skull beneath. Then with a pencil flash he examined both ears and nostrils. Last of all he explored the gunman's half open mouth, withdrawing a dental plate. He made no sound but Blake sensed his triumph as he freed from underside of the plastic denture a small disc which he wrapped in his handkerchief and stowed away in an inner pocket.

"Care to wash now?" Blake asked casually.

Kittson stiffened. He looked up, straight into Blake's eyes. And his own eyes were strange ones—almost yellow, unblinking, like those of some hunting feline. he low, unblinking. like those of some hunting feline. They continued to bore into Blake—or to try to—but he met stare with stare. The agent got to his feet.

"I would, for a fact," his voice was mild, deceptively so, Blake believed. He was certain that in some way he had surprised the man, had failed to respond as the other had expected him to.

When Kittson was wiping his hands there came a knock at the door.

"My men," the agent appeared as certain of that as if he could see through the wall. Blake unlocked and opened the door.

Two men stood outside. Under any other circumstances Blake might not have given them a second glance, but now he watched them with double intentness.

One was almost as tall as Kittson and his wide boned, freckled face was surmounted by a thatch of bright red hair only partially concealed by his hat. The other, in contrast, was not only short but small, delicately boned, almost fail. They gave Blake flickering glances as they passed him, and he felt as though he had been measured, catalogued and filed for all time.

"Okay, chief?" asked the red haired one.

Kittson stepped aside to reveal the man on the floor. "He's all yours, boys——"

Between them they brought the gunman to partial

consciousness and took him out. But Kittson remained and, when they were gone, locked the door for the second time.

Blake watched this move with raised eyebrows. "I assure you," he kept his tone light, "I have no connection with the departed."

"I am sure you have not. However—"

"This is a matter which should not concern me—is that it?"

For the first time Kittson's tight lips moved in a shadow smile. "Just so. We would rather no one knew about this little episode."

"My foster father was on the police force. I don't talk out of turn."

"You are from out of town?"

"I'm from Ohio, yes. My foster parents are dead. I came here to enter Havers," Blake answered with the exact truth.

"Havers—so you are an art student?"

"I have hopes," Blake refused to be drawn. "But five minutes of checking on your part will support all my statements."

Kittson's shadow smile broadened. "I don't doubt that at all, young man. But tell me one thing—just why did you open your door at that crucial moment? I'll swear you couldn't have heard us coming up the corridor, not through these walls and—" He was frowning now, watching Blake with that same hunting cat intensity, as if the young man presented a problem which must be solved.

Blake lost a fraction of his assurance. How could he possibly explain those queer flashes of foreboding, which he had had at intervals all his life, warning him of danger to come? How could he explain to this man that he had been sitting in the dark for at least an hour certain that trouble was ahead and that action on his part was necessary?

Then, moved perhaps by that unblinking, demanding stare, he plunged: "I just had a feeling that something was wrong—that I must open the door."

And those tawny eyes held his as if they would bore into his skull and lay bare every one of his thoughts. Suddenly he resented that suggestion of invasion, and found he was able to break away from that odd hold, that compulsion.

But to his surprise Kittson was nodding. "I'll buy that, Walker. I've faith in hunches. Well, it was a good thing for me that yours—" He paused, froze into immobility except for a gesture with one hand which held Blake as quiet. Kittson might be listening, but thought Blake strained his own ears he could hear nothing at all.

A second later there wes a discreet tap at the door. Blake got up. Kittson was as still as a hunter waiting for prey to come within striking distance. But his head turned to Blake and he shaped words with such exaggerated lip movements that the younger man could read them,

"Ask who?"

Blake went to the door, his hand dropped to the catch but he did not release it as he asked, "Who's there?"

"Hotel security officer." The reply was prompt, only slightly muffled by the barrier. A hand came over his shoulder with a scrap of paper. Block letters read, "Say— check with desk."

"Let me check with the desk," Blake called. He flattened himself against the door. There was no objection, no answer from without. But, after a moment, Blake heard the faint footfalls of someone moving away. He went back to his seat on the bed.

Kittson had preempted the single comfortable chair and was gazing out into the air shaft as if he found the brickwork beyond of absorbing interest.

"I take it that that was *not* the hotel dick?"

12

"No, he was not. Which puts us all in a jam of sorts."
Kittson took out a cigarette case, offered its contents to
Blake, and snapped a lighter for them both. "That was an
attempt to discover what had happened here. Unfortu-
nately it means that you have now been linked with us.
And that leads to complications all around.

"There are good and sufficient reasons why we do not
want our actions to become public. We shall have to ask
you to cooperate with us."

Blake stirred. "I'm just an innocent bystander. I didn't
come here to play cops and robbers. And I'm not even
asking what I'm mixed up in—which I believe shows
some restraint on my part." Again Kittson smiled faintly
and Blake continued, "I just want to go about my own
business. . . ."

Kittson tossed his hat on the desk and leaned back his
black head to blow a perfect smoke ring. "And we'd like
nothing better than to see you do just that. But I'm afraid
it's too late for second thoughts now. You should have
had those before you opened your door. Others have
taken an interest in you, and that might prove—at the
best—embarrassing. At the worst—" his eyes glinted like
gem stones through the smoke and Blake felt an odd
chill, almost a suspicion of that same uneasiness which
had drawn him into this adventure. Kittson was implying
things, and the force of his implications was heightened
by the very vagueness of his words.

"I see that it begins to dawn on you that this is serious.
When must you report at Havers for classes?"

"The new term begins next Monday."

"A week. I'm going to ask you to play along with us for
that period. If we have any luck this case will be settled
by then, or at least your part of it will. Otherwise—"

"Otherwise I might be taken care of for my own good
and yours?" Blake demanded. But he recognized the
voice of authority. This man was used to giving orders

which were obeyed without question. If he said "Remove Blake Walker and put him on ice," Blake Walker would be removed with the same speed and efficiency as the gunman had earlier been extracted from this room. No one ever gained by ramming a stone wall head on. Better follow orders—at least until he could learn more about the setup.

"All right. What do I do?"

"You vanish. Here and now. How much luggage do you have?"

Kittson was on his feet, across the room to open the closet before Blake really understood that reply to his question.

"One bag." Something, perhaps the power of the other's personality swept Blake into action he would not have considered an hour before. He snapped the suitcase shut and took out his wallet to count out some bills on the top of the chest.

"I take it that we do *not* check out-formally." It was more a statement than a question and he was not surprised as Kittson swiftly agreed.

The gray light outside the window had brightened very little. It was five minutes after seven, but the dusk within the room was that of evening as the agent snapped off the light. Blake shrugged into his top coat, picked up his hat and bag, ready to follow as the other beckoned him out into the hall.

They did not take the turn leading to the elevator, but instead went to a firedoor. Stairs, five floors of them, silent and deserted as the hall had been—then Kittson paused for a moment before another door, giving the impression of listening. Down another flight of stairs, narrower, not so well lighted, threading through a place of storage compartments to more steps going up. They emerged on the open street with the chill drizzle of sleet in their faces. Blake was sure that his guide not only knew exactly where he was going, but that they had been unobserved throughout that flight. His belief in the efficiency of the agent's organization was settled for all time as a taxi came in at the curb almost as they crossed the strip of pavement. Kittson opened the door and Blake obeyed the implied order. But to his surprise the agent did not join him. Instead the door slammed shut and the cab pulled away.

For the moment Blake was content to follow orders and see where all this stage managing would leave him. But, as he had more time to think and was out of the range of Kittson's electric personality, he was surprised at his own compliance with every suggestion the agent had made. If this wasn't some weird dream it came very close to it. Undoubtedly the wisest thing for him to do would be to stop this cab and disappear on his own. Only he had a very strong suspicion that Kittson would sooner or later catch up with him again and that then their relationship would be on a far less easy footing.

The taxi wove through the narrow roads in the central park in a shuttle pattern which completely baffled Blake's scant knowledge of the city. Then they came out on the main streets once more. Morning traffic was on the move and the cab rounded busses, bored between trucks and private cars. It slowed at last to whip into a narrow alley running between blank walled buildings which might be warehouses. About three-quarters of the way down this the driver pulled to a stop.

"Here y'are."

Blake reached for his wallet. But the driver said, without turning around, "It's already paid, Mac. You go in that door, see? Elevator there. Punch the top button. Now make it snappy, Mac, this here's no place to park!"

Blake went on in to be confronted by the glass frosted panel of a self-operating elevator. He punched the top button and tried to count the floors as he moved upward creakily, but he was not sure whether they came to stop before nine or ten.

Beyond was a scrap of hall, hardly more than standing room before a single blank door. Blake knocked and the portal opened so speedily that he thought they must have been awaiting him.

"Come in, Walker."

Blake had been expecting Kittson. But the man who greeted him was the elder of the agent by at least ten years. He was shorter and his hair was brindled with gray threads among the dark brown. But, as inconspicuous as he might have been in a crowd, there was a quiet distinction in his air. He was as much a personality in his way as the more aggressive Kittson.

"I am Jason Saxton," he introduced himself. "And Mark Kittson is waiting. Just leave your things here."

Deftly separated from coat, hat and bag, Blake was ushered into an inner office where he found not only Kittson but the red haired man who had helped remove the gunman in the Shelborne.

The room was bare except for a wall range of files, a desk and three or four chairs. There was not even a window to break the gray walls, matched in shade by a carpet under foot. And the lighting came from a concealed source near the ceiling.

"This is Hoyt," Kittson indicated the redhead abruptly. "You made the trip without incident, I see."

Blake wanted to ask what kind of an "incident" Kittson had expected him to encounter, but he decided that his wisest move now was to let the other fellow do the talking.

Hoyt was slumped down in his chair, his long legs stretched out, his hands, with their fringing of coarse red hairs, finger-laced across his flat middle.

"Joey knows his stuff," he observed lazily. "Stan will report if anyone showed undue interest."

16

"I believe you said your father was a policeman. Where? In Ohio?" Kittson paid no attention to his colleague's comment.

"In Columbus, yes. But I said my foster father," corrected Blake. He was on guard, aware that every word he spoke was being noted, weighed by all of the three fronting him.

"And your real parents?"

Blake told his story in as few words as possible. Hoyt might have dozed off during that recital, his eyes were closed. Saxton gave it the courteous attention a personnel man would grant that of a job applicant. And Kittson continued to study him with those hard, amber eyes.

"That's it," he ended.

Hoyt arose in one lithe and strangely graceful movement. His eyes, now fully opened, Blake noticed, were green, as vivid in color and as compelling when he turned them on one, as were Kittson's.

"I take it Walker is staying?" he asked of the room at large.

Instinctively Blake glanced at Kittson; the final decision lay with the agent he was sure. And on the desk he now noticed something new. In the middle of the green blotter was a small ball of crystal. Some movement of the agent's must have disturbed it for it began to roll toward Blake. It had almost reached the edge of the desk when he put out his hand and caught it.

CHAPTER TWO

Its weight suggested that it was a natural crystal. But when he reached out to replace it on the desk there was a change in it. He had caught a clear ball, what he now

17

held was a globe in which swirled a blue-green twist of vapour. As he continued to hold it that vapour grew more dense, thickened, until the color was solid.

The change was uncanny. Blake set it down as if the ball seared his flesh. Now the blue-green was fading once more. But Saxton was on his feet, crowding forward against Hoyt to watch the transformation. Kittson's hand covered the sphere. The blue-green was gone. But had there been the beginning of another change? The agent dropped the globe into a drawer. Not before Blake was certain that in a few short seconds that the other's fingers had been in contact with the crystal an orange-red mist had begun to collect within. Before he could ask a question a warning buzz from a plate set in the wall was an interuption.

There followed the hum of the elevator and Hoyt answered the door, admitting his small comrade of the early morning.

"Everything satisfactory?" That was Kittson.

"Yes," the voice was light, musical. He might have been a boy hardly out of his teens, until you saw his eyes, assessed the very faint lines about his almost-too-well shaped mouth. "There was a tail: that squat punk from the Crystal Bird. You'd think they wouldn't use the same men so often."

"The supply of proper material may be strictly limited," suggested Saxton.

"For which we should give thanks," Kittson caught him up. "One raid, if we could be sure of getting all the dupes together, would put our friend out of business here."

"To send him hopping," Saxton's slow voice was clearly warning. "Better keep him on this level." His eyes touched Blake and he was abruptly silent.

The young man who had just come in shrugged out of his coat and draped it across a chair. "Roscoe isn't too bright. I left him nosing a cold trail. We needn't worry about him for an hour or so. Walker's in the clear for the time being."

Kittson leaned back in his chair. "That may be. But they'll back track on him when it dawns that he's given them the slip." He turned to Blake. "Did you tell anyone at the hotel that you were going to attend classes at Havers?"

"The doorman. I asked him about a bus to get out there. But he's used to questions about transportation; he must be asked a hundred a day. He won't remember just one."

The others, by their expressions, did not agree with that hope.

"People have a way of recalling just what you want them to forget, when it is made clear to them that it is important," Kittson remarked. "We'll keep you here a couple of days, until we can assess the amount of excitement your disappearance causes—that's the only way to check their interest in you. Sorry, Walker. You need not remind me that this action is undue interference in your private life. I know that as well as you do. But sometimes situations develop when innocent bystanders have to suffer for the general good. We can give you comfortable quarters and your stay is for your own protection as well as for the safety of our investigation."

"I think," Saxton got up, "that our first gesture of hospitality might be to offer breakfast."

And Blake, rising to that bait readily enough, followed him through the second door in the office into an astonishing suite of rooms. The furniture was modern in monotones of gray, green and odd, misty shades of blue. There were no pictures and in each room the lighting came from the ceiling. A TV set of some size stood against one wall and a great many books, papers and current magazines were profusely scattered in piles on tables, and stacks on the floor, within easy reach of each chair.

"Our quarters are a little cramped," his host informed him. "You will have to share my sleeping accommodations, I'm afraid. In here—" He opened a door off a short hall to display a sizeable room with twin beds.

"And here breakfast awaits."

There were no windows. Blake puzzled over that as he took his place at a table and Saxton went to the wall, pushed aside a panel and lifted out a tray which he put before his guest, bringing out a second for himself.

It was a hearty meal, excellently prepared, and Blake enjoyed it. Saxton smiled.

"This is one of the cook's generous mornings." He pushed aside a pile of books.

They were all histories, some English and some American, and they bristled with small paper markers as if some program of intensive research was underway. Saxton indicated them.

"They represent a hobby of mine, Walker. It is also, in a manner of speaking, connected with my employment. You are perhaps yourself a student of history?"

Blake took time to think as he swallowed a bite of ham. Either he was jumpy or Saxton had purpose behind this line of conversation.

"My foster father collected books on criminal history—famous trials, things like that. I read those—and diaries and letters—Pepys-eyewitness accounts."

Saxton held his coffee cup poised, studying it as if it had suddenly turned into a precious bit of antique china. "Eyewitness reports-just so. Tell me, have you ever heard of the 'possibility worlds' theory of history?"

"I've read some fantasy fiction founded on that. You mean that idea that two complete worlds stem from every momentous historical decision? One in which Napoleon won the Battle of Waterloo, say, and our own in which he lost it?"

"Yes. There would be myriad worlds, all influenced by

various decisions. Not only by the obvious ones of battles and political changes, but even by the appearance and use of certain inventions. A fascinating supposition."

Blake nodded. Sure, the idea was interesting, and it was manifestly Saxton's hobbyhorse. But at the present moment he was more absorbed by the predicament of one Blake Walker and *his* possibility worlds.

"There are points of departure even within the past few years," the man across the table was continuing. "Conceive a world in which Hitler won the Battle of Britain and overran England in 1941. Suppose a great leader is born too early or too late."

Blake's interest was sparked. "I read a short story about that once," he agreed. "How a British diplomat in the early 1790s met a retired Major of artillery dying in a small French town—Napoleon born too soon."

"But suppose," Saxton had set down his cup and now he leaned forward his eyes alight, "suppose such a man, born out of his time in his own world, were given the ability to move from one possibility line to another— would he not be doubly dangerous? Suppose you were born in an era in which your own society stifled your particular talents, giving you, as you thought, no proper outlet."

"You'd then move to where you could use them." That was elementary. But Saxton was beaming at him as if he had been a bright pupil coming out of a quiz with honors. There was definitely something behind all this— what? His warning sense had not been alerted, but he had a feeling that he was being carefully steered along a path Saxton had chosen for him and that it was being done under orders.

"That might be a good idea," he added.

But that was *not* the right answer this time.

"For *you*," Saxton rapped out. "But perhaps not for the

21

world you moved to. That presents another side to the problem doesn't it? Ha! Erskine! Come and join us."

"Any coffee left?" It was the slender, blond man. "No? Well, press the button, Jas. I need reviving after a rugged morning."

When he dropped onto the bench beside his older colleague he smiled at Blake, a flash which wiped the boredom from his face and gave his well-cut features warmth and life.

"We're to stick around here," he announced. "What did you do with the paper, Jas? I want to see the TV program. If we have to be cooped up we might as well enjoy it."

He removed a fresh jug of coffee from behind the panel and loaded his first cup with two heaping teaspoonsful of sugar. When they returned to the sitting room Erskine seated himself before the TV. There was something odd in his absorbtion in the very ordinary entertainment offered, almost as if TV were a new toy which enchanted him. As the program signed off he sighed.

"Amazing appeal for such primitive stuff—"

Blake caught that murmur. But the show had not been some ancient movie. It was a "live" and fairly well done production. Why the application of "primitive"? There were tiny threads of "wrongness." A suspicion triggered by Saxton's table conversation crossed Blake's mind only to be smothered by sane reason.

They were undistrubed for the rest of the day and evening 'though without windows it was difficult to say whether it was day or night. Erksine and Saxton played a card game which blake was sure he had never seen before. They ate heartily of the meals which came from behind the panel and Blake browsed amid the wealth of reading matter. It was predominately historical or biographical in subject. And the spiking of reference slips continued from book to book. Was Saxton planing to write an article on his hobby? Blake continued to think about the problem the other had proposed that morning.

A man born out of his time on his own world, but able to visit a new one in which his particular talents could bring him the power he craved. He found himself producing some fantasies of his own based on that.

Who were his companions, or maybe it should be *what* were they? He was still thinking lazily of that as he drifted off to sleep some hours later.

He awoke in the dark. There was no sound from the other bed. Blake wriggled out from between the covers and investigated. The other bed was rumpled but empty. He went to the door and opened it a crack.

Kittson, one arm about Saxton's shoulders, was being supported down the hall. There was a dark stain on his shirt and his feet stumbled as he went. A moment later both men passed through the door at the far end and it closed. But on the carpet a shiny spot rested like a coin. Blake stooped to touch it and his finger came away both wet and red. Blood!

He was still waiting for Saxton to return when sleep overcame him. When he roused again, the lights were aglow and the other bed was smoothly made. Blake dressed hurriedly. Kittson had been hurt, but why the secrecy?

As he went out into the hall he looked for the stain. It was gone as he had thought it would be. But when he ran his fingers over the pile they detected dampness. Someone had made a thorough job of cleaning, and not long ago. It was now he consulted his watch, half-past eight, Tuesday morning. And he had some questions to ask.

Jason Saxton was alone in the living room, a topheavy pile of volumes resting on the coffee table before him, a secretary's notebook half-filled with minute script on his knee. He glanced up with a smile so open that Blake curbed his impatience.

"I hope that I did not disturb you this morning, Walker. We're short-handed and I'm to take over the office. So you'll be more or less left to yourself today."

Blake murmured an agreement and went on to the dining room. Erskine was there before him. His smooth face was drawn and tired, and there were brown smudges under his heavy-lidded eyes. He grunted something that might have been a greeting, and waved a hand at the panel. Blake withdrew a tray and sat down to eat, leaving it to the other to initiate conversation. But Erskine was apparently not one of those souls who felt their brightest in the morning. After he drank his coffee he got up.

"Have fun!" he bade Blake almost sardonically.

"I shall," the other assured him. And then wondered if he had given his plans away by his inflection. He was almost sure Erskine had shot a doubtful glance at him before he left the room.

Blake lingered over the meal, wanting to have the apartment to himself for his own purposes. He made sure the office door was closed behind both men when he readied for action.

In the center of the living room he stood still, listening. Then he crossed to put his ear to the panel of the outer door. He could hear, very faintly the murmur of voices, followed by the opening and closing of file drawers. A rumble—surely that was the elevator. Cautiously he tried the door and was not in the least surprised to find it locked.

Blake went back to the hall off which opened the bedrooms and got down on his knees. There was more than one damp spot in the carpet. And they led to the door through which Kittson had been helped the night before. This, too, was locked and he could hear no sound from beyond. But the next room was open for his inspection and it was very similar to the one he shared with Saxton. Both beds were smoothly made; there was no sign of luggage. Bureau drawers opened to display neat and innocent piles of clean shirts and underwear, socks and neckties.

There were an unusual number of suits in the closet and they ranged from well-cut tweeds, through ultra-conservative business wear, to levis and semi-uniforms such as delivery men might use. Apparently the inhabitants of the apartment were sartorially equipped for every occasion. Well, that might be demanded of F.B.I. agents. As yet he had discovered nothing to suggest that they were not exactly what Kittson claimed them to be.

But Blake was not satisfied. He found a small automatic in the drawer of a night table. But that could not be evidence of what he sought. The few toilet articles were well-known brands such as could be bought in any drug store. He did note hair dye which again could be easily explained.

After ten minutes he had searched all the easily accessible places. Dare he really tear the place apart without leaving any evidence of his investigations? He was sure, after surveying the meticulous neatness of the bed making, that he could not. But he did empty every drawer and turn it upside down to see if anything had been taped to bottom or sides. The worst of it was that he had no idea of what he was looking for except that he wanted some concrete answer to certain fantastic suspicions.

He went through Saxton's half of his own room with the same thoroughness, finding nothing. After that he did not try to search the living room but he did check the office door; it was still locked and very quiet as if Saxton, too, had now gone out.

No one joined him for lunch, and boredom drove him to the books. He could not rid himself of speculations concerning Saxton's time traveler, inventing a few possibility worlds which might attract such a man. How would it feel to step into another such level? Suddenly he was cold, chilled and apprehensive. What had seemed an exercise of the imagination began to take on sinister connotations.

It was easy enough to accept the idea of a civilization being upset by a single man with an overwhelming belief in his own destiny and a power of character; his world had had its share of earthshakers and movers native born. The driving force of those men had been a vicious appetite for power.

And that was a human drive right enough. Unite it to the supreme type of egotism which does not brook any opposition and you get a Napoleon, an Alexander, a Caesar, the Khans who almost smashed Europe as well as Asia.

And picture such a man frustrated in his own world but able to move on to one ripe for his rise! Suppose that *had* happened in the past. Blake reined in his imagination and forced a laugh which echoed too hollowly in the silent room. But he did not wonder at Saxton's absorption with the theory.

He put aside his book and stretched out on the wide couch. It was getting on into the afternoon. Would they let him go by Friday? Hush-hush stuff. Grade-B spy thriller.

His mind and body tensed. He stared up unseeingly at the ceiling. Something was on the way. All that warning which had been pulling at him in the hotel yesterday was now flooding back a hundred fold. Vague discomfort shaped speedily into the sensation of being hunted, of danger approaching.

Blake sat up, but he did not stoop to put on his shoes. This was stronger, in its way worse, than any of the attacks he had known before.

He went down the hall to the door through which Kittson had gone. The last time he had experienced this it had been associated with the agent. The door was still locked. He rattled the knob, knocked as his discomfort grew. There was no answer from within.

Blake returned to the living room and there the menace was intensified. As a weathercock influenced by an unseen wind he wheeled toward the office door, pressing against it, very sure that whatever was coming had its source in that direction.

He not only heard the rumble of the elevator but felt the vibration of its rise. Its passenger must now be in the small hall outside the office. Was Saxton waiting to receive the invader?

It was in that moment, without knowing just why, Blake ranged himself on the side of the four men whose quarters he now shared. They had told him very little; there was much which needed explanation—yet now he was one with them, and this newcomer could only be defined as the enemy.

There was no click of the door, no movement within the office. Then he caught the faintest of scratching sounds as if someone were working at the lock. It lasted for only a moment. The stranger might be as intent upon listening as Blake was.

But he was totally unprepared for what followed. Suddenly he was conscious of an intangible presence, a personality without body or substance. It was as if that other listener had projected an emanation of himself past the barrier he could not force. Through that utter silence the intrusion provoked panic.

Blake backed away from the door, some inner core rebelling against possible contact with that—that Thing! But a second later he returned to his post, positive that if the other got into the office physically, he was going to know it.

For a space that weird sensation of another's presence persisted. But he was certain that it was not yet in turn aware of his occupancy of the room. He was becoming adjusted to it, able to relax for a second, when, with a cat's leap it struck straight at him.

Blake's hand went to his head. Contact had come as sharply as a blow, a blow which addled coherent thought. With the other hand he clung to the door knob, with a queer feeling that that one sane and ordinary object between his fingers would keep him safe against that foul onslaught.

For, having once established touch, the thing—power —personality—however it could be identified, attacked viciously. It was a spike ground in between Blake's eyes, striving to force a path to his brain.

As he held to the knob with a frenzied grip, gray blurs of pain veiling the room, his body shook with long nervous shudders. No physical torture, he thought, could ever equal this. He was meeting a test as out of place in his time and world as the personal Devil of the middle ages might be.

The agonizing pressure faded, but Blake did not dare to believe that it was retreating for good. And his refusal to believe in escape was justified, the other had not abandoned battle. For the attack swept in a second time, prying, biting in search of an easy victory.

CHAPTER THREE

BLAKE endured as the floor rolled in sickening waves under his feet. There was no measure of time. He could only hold to reason and sanity typified by the door knob sticky with his sweat.

He was dully surprised that his ears could still catch

the sound which brought an abrupt end to that malevolent assault: the buzz of the warning within the office. There was an instant withdrawal on the part of the enemy. Blake heard the sound of the elevator.

Erskine or Saxton returning? If so, were they about to walk in unwarned upon the danger lurking out there? There was nothing he could do, no way he could prevent it.

The elevator bumped to a stop, paused, and then began a jerky descent. And it took with it the presence which had haunted the room. The whine thinned, to be followed by utter silence—that other had gone.

Blake was on his knees, his forehead resting against the door, his stomach churning. He started to crawl. With the aid of the nearest chair he got to his feet and staggered on, making the bathroom just in time. Weak with retching, he leaned against the wall. For the worst of that attack had been the feeling of being utterly befouled.

When he could keep his feet he pulled off his clothing and stepped into the shower. Only when the water had alternately cooked and frozen his flesh for long moments did he begin to feel clean once more. Dressing was a task. He was as tired as if he were moving about for the first time after a long and serious illness.

Blake wavered out into the living room to collapse on the couch. So far he had concentrated on the obvious, on being wretchedly sick, on bathing and dressing. His mind refused to be pushed beyond those immediate actions. But now to think about it made him sick again. He began to repeat random lines of poetry, slogans, anything with rhythm. But between one word and another, oozing over and through and by those lines his lips shaped, he recalled painfully that strange attack. He was alone now; he would swear to that. And yet the invisible slime left by that visitor was thick in the air he drew into his lungs. He could almost smell its stench.

That sound—the elevator again! Blake tried to sit up. The walls whirled. He clawed wildly at the fabric of the couch. Then he blacked out.

He awakened in his bed, hungry and oddly alert from the second of returning consciousness. From somewhere came the murmur of voices. Het got up. Doors were open in the hall and he listened without shame.

"... canvassed the whole town, up, down and sidewise. His story is true. Foster child of the Walkers. Found in an alley by two cops ... the whole fantastic thing. He's well enough liked but he seems to have no very close friends." There was no mistaking Hoyt's drawl.

"Found in an alley—" Saxton sounded thoughtful. "I wonder. Yes, I do wonder."

"Any signs of substitution and erasure, or applied false memories?" Kittson's demand cut through.

"Nobody I met showed them. I don't see how he could possibly be a plant—"

"Not a plant, no," that was Saxton again. "But perhaps something else. We aren't all knowing. No close friends. If what we suspect is true, that would inevitably follow. And the evidence of the selector was certainly empathic enough. We can't afford yet to take the position of 'who I don't know is against me.' And he did come to Mark's aid at the Shelborne."

"Just how do you rate him, Jas?" Erskine asked.

"Latent psi, of course. Which bothers him as it naturally would. Intelligent with something else I can not put name to yet. What are you going to do with him, Mark?"

"What I'd like to know," Erskine again, "is what happened here this afternoon. He'd blacked out; perfectly limp when we found him. Took both of us to stow him in bed."

"What would happen if a psi with the sort of barrier that lad naturally possessed met a mind probe?" Kittson inquired with chill dryness.

30

"But that would mean—!" Saxton's voice was a shrill protest.

"Certainly. And we'd better begin thinking about Pranj's being able to do just that. I want to ask that young man some questions as soon as he is awake. You did give him a restorer shot?"

"About third strength," Saxton assented. "After all, I'm not sure of the reactions of his race. I'm not even sure about his race." The last sentence might have been a thought spoken aloud.

Blake walked into the room. All four of them eyed him without surprise.

"What do you want to ask me?" he spoke to Kittson.

"What happened here this afternoon?"

Choosing his words carefully, trying to keep all emotion out of it, Blake detailed his adventure. There was no disbelief around that circle. A little of his belligerence ebbed. Were they *used* to such attacks? If so, what in the world—or who in the world—was this quartette of hunters trailing?

"Mind probe," Kittson was definite. "You are sure he did not physically enter the office?"

"As sure as I can be without having watched him."

"Well, Stan?" Kittson's attention shifted to the boyish Erskine who was curled up on the coach.

The slight blond man nodded. "I told you Pranj was an adept. He did a lot of experimenting the Hundred never knew about. That's why he's so deadly. If Walker hadn't been psi, and a barrier psi at that, he'd have sucked him dry like this!" He snapped his fingers.

"What is psi?" Blake broke in, determined to have a few answers which would make sense as far as he was concerned.

"Psi—parapsychological powers—is extrasensory preception in different fields, abilities which mankind as a whole has not yet learned to exploit." Saxton had turned schoolmaster again. "Telepathy—the communication between one mind and another without the need for oral speech; Telekinesis—transportation of material objects by power of will; Clairvoyance—witnessing of events occuring at a distance! Pervision—foretelling of events to come; Levitation—the ability to move one's body through the air—these are phenomena which have been recognized in part. And such attributes may be latent in an individual; unless he is pushed by circumstances into using them, he may not know that he possesses psi abilities."

"Why," Kittson broke into the lecture, "did you open your door on Monday morning, Walker—just at the right moment for me?"

Blake answered with the truth. "Because I thought that I had to—"

"Did that compulsion come suddenly?" Saxton wanted to know.

Black shook his head. "No. I'd been feeling—well, uneasy for about an hour. It always works that way."

"Then you've had it before. Does it always foretell danger?"

"Yes. But not danger to me—or at least not always."

"And afterwards," Kittson was addressing Saxton now, "I was unable to take him over because of his natural shield."

"I don't see why we should be surprised," Hoyt contributed for the first time. "It stands to reason that since we were the same stock in the beginning, we're going to discover latents here and there. We're lucky that so far we haven't run into any true power men—"

"Do you mean," Blake selected his words carefully, "that all of you have such powers and can use them at will?"

For a long moment they were silent, the other three looking to Kittson as if waiting his decision. He shrugged.

"He knows too much; we'll have to take him all the

way. If Pranj's men pick him up now . . . And we can't keep him under wraps forever, though this is beginning to look like a long term job." He held out his hand and the package of cigarettes lying near Erskine's knee floated lightly across several feet of space to make a neat landing on his palm.

"Yes, we have control over some psi powers. The degree varies as to the person and his training. Some are better telepaths than telekinesists. We have a few teleports—people able to project themselves from one point to another. Precognition is common to a degree—"

"And you *aren't* F.B.I. agents!" Blake added.

"No, not agents of the F.B.I. We *are* members of another law enforcement body, perhaps just now more important to the well being of this world. We are Wardsmen. Jas has told you of the possibility worlds, only it isn't his hobby or only a theory but cold fact. There are bands, levels, whatever you wish to call them, of worlds. This world has been reproduced innumerable times by historical events. My race is no older than yours, but by some chance we developed an extremely mechanized civilization several thousand years ago.

"Unfortunately we possessed the common human trait of combativeness and the result was an appalling atomic war. Why we did not end by blowing ourselves out of existence as other level worlds have done and are doing right now, we shall never know. But instead of total destruction, the result, for a handful of widely scattered survivors, was a new type of life. Probably the second generation after the war was largely mutant, but we learned to use psi powers.

"War was outlawed. We turned our energy to the conquest of space, only to discover that the planets in our system were largely inimical to man. Expeditions left for the stars—none have yet returned. Then one of our historian-scientists discovered the levels of 'Successor

33

Worlds' as we term them. Travel, not backward or forward in time, but across it, became common. And, because we are human, trouble developed too. It was necessary to keep a check on irresponsible travelers, prevent criminals from looting on other time lines where their powers gave them vast advantage. Thus the organization we represent came into being.

"We maintain order among travelers but in no way may we interfere with action on another level. Before we take a case we are given a complete briefing on language, history, customs of the level on which we must operate. Some levels are forbidden to any one except official observers. Others no one dares to enter—civilization—or the lack of it—there has taken such a twist that it is unsafe.

"There are dead, radio-active worlds, worlds foul with man-made plagues, worlds held in subjection under governments so vicious that their inhabitants are no longer strictly human. Then there are others where civilization is poised on a trigger edge, where the mere presence of an outsider might wreck the status quo.

"Which brings us to the case now in point. We are after—well, by the standards of our culture he is a criminal. Kmoat Vo Pranj is one of those super egos who craves power as an addict craves his drug. We no longer have nationalty divisions within our world, but we do have differences of race due to barriers caused by the atomic war of the past. Saxton and I represent a group descended from members of a military unit which was cut off for several hundred years in the extreme north on this continent. Hoyt's ancestors took to living underground in that island known to you as Great Britain, developing a separate culture of their own. While Erskine, like the man we hunt, is a member of a third grouping, limited to less than a million, all springing from a handful of technicians who remained in a compact community in the South American mountains, working for expert control of psi powers."

"In addition to which," Erskine's voice was colorless, remote," we also produce from time to time variations of the stock who have the unpleasant natures of our remote warlord ancestors. Pranj wants a world to conquer. Not being able to realize that ambition on our level, in fact now that he is recognized for what he is, he will be subjected to corrective treatment, he seeks an outlet for his energy elsewhere. He played the role of a normal so well that he was able to enter our Service and mastered training to the point of level travel without supervision.

"Now he is in search of a level where civilization is ready to allow him full scope. Having found such a world, he will build up an organization and make himself ruler of the planet. Part of his unbalance is a super self-confidence. He lacks all elements of self-doubt, remorse or any softer virtue. Our purpose is not only to take him into custody but to repair any damage he might have already done."

"You think he is here—right here?" Blake had passed the point of accepting or not accepting the fantastic story; he was merely listening.

"You may have met him this afternoon—if not face to face," was Erskine's sober and apparently sane reply.

Kittson produced a small cube of some clear substance. For a moment it rested on his palm, then it lifted, to sail across to the hand Blake extended rather gingerly. Through the clear envelope he looked down at a tiny figure, bright with color, glowing with a life-like hue as if the cube did encase a living manikin. The tiny man had the same sharply marked cheekbones, delicately cut thin lips, blond hair which were Erskine's. But there was in addition a subtle difference and the longer Blake studied the figure the more marked that difference became. Erskine was aloof, his air of detachment must be inborn, yet one sensed that there was no malice, no assumption of superiority in his manner. This statuette was of a man who was ruthless. There was a shadow about the corners of the lips, a slight shade about the eyes. It was a cruel face, an arrogant face, and a very powerful one.

"That is Pranj—or rather as Pranj was before he disappeared," Kittson explained. "What type of disguise or cover he may have assumed we do not yet know. We have to locate him in spite of it."

"Is he working alone?"

Hoyt shook his head. "You met one of his dupes at the Shelborne. He has recruits, none of whom, we think, know the real truth. He provides some of them with varied gadgets which tend to make it harder for us."

"Any one of us," Kittson took up the explanation, "can master mentally the types Pranj draws to him, if they are unshielded. That thug in the hotel was wearing a shield to protect his mind against mine."

"That disc you found in his mouth?"

"Just so. Luckily an essential ingredient in those can be obtained only on our level. And Pranj can not have too many to scatter around."

"Let us get back to this afternoon," Erskine cut in. "I think we can be sure Pranj made us a visit. Somebody used a probe on Walker and we didn't. Pranj—do you agree?"

Saxton sighed. "We must move. Such a pity."

"But we are lucky in this much," Erskine had not finished. "What if he had come when all of us were gone? We might never have known until too late that he had spotted this place. So we're ahead there. What about it, Mark, do we move?"

"Yes. I'm sure that this level world is his main objective. If he is hopping for safety, he'll come back to fight. And he can't have his way here until he removes us, a job which we shall make as difficult as possible. Now," he turned to Blake, "it's up to you. Frankly, you know too much for our comfort. You'll *have* to come in with us."

Blake stared down at the carpet. Big of them to offer him a choice, he thought wryly. He did not doubt that he would be efficiently dealt with if he said "no." But after this afternoon he found that he had not the slightest idea of replying in the negative.

"I agree."

They accepted that without thanks or comment. He might have said that it was a pleasant night out. And then he was forgotten as Kittson gave orders:

"We'll move tomorrow after Jas has a chance to check on number two. Hoyt, you patrol the Crystal Bird beat. There's no hope of getting at him there, but try and discover how many of the attendant goons are wearing shields. Erskine—"

The blond man shook his head. "I've a job of my own. Today I thought I spotted a Ming-Hawn throat jewel in one of those antique jewelry shops along the parkway. The store was closed, so I'll have to make sure the first thing in the morning."

"Ming-Hawn!" Saxton's voice trailed off into a breathy hiss.

Kittson studied a smoke ring. "Might be. If Pranj's hard up for ready cash, a few things of that nature sold in the right places would be a good fund raising project."

"But any expert seeing it would ask questions! And he doesn't want exposure any more than we do!" protested the other.

"I don't know about exposure. Not all Ming-Hawn pieces are so distinctive that they would be recognized as alien art. You weren't absolutely sure yourself, were you, Stan?"

"Almost certain. I want to handle it. But it's worth investigating. Suppose I take Walker with me."

For one anxious moment Blake was afraid that Kittson

would refuse. But reluctant or not, the agent finally agreed. And when he woke in the morning, after a dream-filled night, Blake was aware of an inner excitement which was not a warning.

With Erskine he descended to the basement of the building, traversed a dingy pawn shop there. The proprietor of this daw's nest did not even look up as they went out his front door. They reached the corner just in time to swing on board a bus. Before they had gone five blocks they were in another section of town with wider streets and smarter shops. And having crossed to thriving intersections Erskine signalled to leave the bus.

"Second from the corner."

The shop Erskine indicated was aristocratically somber in black and gold paint. There was a wrought iron grill covering the lower part of the show window to protect but not conceal the display within. Erskine pointed to a piece close to the glass.

It was a pendant of a silvery metal set with discs of black, on the surface of each of which were intricate patterns in enamels. There was something vaguely oriental about the piece and yet Blake could not place it as belonging to any Eastern art he had ever seen.

"Ming-Hawn right enough. We've got to find out how it came here."

Erskine went into the shop and addressed the man who had risen from behind a desk to greet them.

"You are Mr. Arthur Beneirs?"

"Yes. There is something I may show you gentlemen?"

"I am told that you buy as well as sell curiosities, Mr. Beneirs?"

The man shook his head. "Not from the general public, sir. I am sometimes called in to bid upon objects which must be sold to settle estates. But otherwise—no."

"You would, however, value an art object?" persisted Erskine.

"Perhaps—"

"This, for example?" Erskine held out the crystal ball Blake had himself held two days before.

"Rock crystal," Beneirs turned it about. But to Blake's amazement this time there was no change in the color of the sphere. It remained clear and uncloudy.

Then, without a word, he put it down, went straight to the window and took out the pendant. When he handed it to Erskine he spoke rapidly, as one reciting a memorized lesson.

"This was brought to me two days ago with other antique jewelry by an attorney, Geoffrey Lake. I have often had dealings with him before in estate sales. He did not tell me from whom he had received it, but I think it was given to him to sell privately. Lake is a man of good reputation—his office is in the Parker Building, suite 140. The price I paid was two hundred and fifty dollars."

Erskine brought out a wallet and counted out some bills. With almost mechanical movements Beneirs picked up the money while Erskine put the piece in his wallet. He then pocketed the crystal. Beneirs, as if they were now invisible, went back to his seat behind the desk, paying no more attention to them.

CHAPTER FOUR

"THERE MUST be some simple explanation for Mr. Beneir's remarkable cooperation," remarked Blake mildly as they went out.

Erskine laughed. "Simple is right. The sphere not only proved that he had no psi powers, but enabled me to take him over and he responded by telling everything he knew. Beneirs won't even remember us. He'll have some vague memory of selling the Ming-Hawn piece, but if he has to report back to this Lake, he will not recall any of the details of the transaction. So now we're one piece ahead in the game, having a line to Lake."

"But what is Ming-Hawn?"

"Who, rather than what. Ming-Hawn was an artist in enamel, a form of art peculiar to his successor world, who did his best work at the end of the 18th century. He inhabited a world which exists as the result of a successful Mongol conquest of all Europe occuring in the thirteenth century. Refugees from that invasion, Norman, Breton, Norse, Saxon, fled westward by ship to Viking colonies in Vinland. Their descendants intermarried with Indians from the spreading native empires in the southwest and formed the nation of Ixanilia which is still in existence on that level. The present civilization is not an attractive one, but it offers possibilities which might attract Pranj. However, now we want Lake."

Erskine turned into a drugstore and made his way to the phone booths. He picked up the classified directory and pushed the other to Blake. "See if his home phone is listed."

Blake was still searching when Erskine made a call. He emerged from the booth frowning.

"Lake's ill—in the hospital. Lives in tho Nelson Arms."

"No number listed there for him," Blake answered.

"Hmmm." Erskine produced a second dime and this time his voice reached Blake faintly from out of the booth.

"Geoffrey Lake, attorney, Nelson Arms. We want the usual report as quick as you can make it. Yes." He hung up. "Now back to our hole-in. This is moving day."

"Somebody will check on Lake?"

"We pay an investigation agency for such routine. If Lake's straight we can work it one way; if he's crooked he may be sitting in Pranj's pocket. Then we'll have to be more cautious."

They did not return through the celler pawn shop, but made their way around the block. Erskine grinned at Blake.

"More than one door to a fox den. You'll have to learn 'em."

"You've a rather elaborate set-up. Wasn't it difficult to arrange?"

"Not so much. In the worlds we visit constantly for trade or study we have permanent bases manned by our people under a good cover. This is a make-shift, but it coincides in space with one of our shift bases and, being a warehouse, it was easy to lease and make our own interior changes."

Erskine led the way into the dingy lobby of a small office building. The white haired man lounging on a stool before the open door of the elevator put aside his tabloid and smiled at Erskine.

" 'Lo, Mr. Waters. Good trip?"

"Fair, Pop. The boss ought to like the sales report. How's the back?"

" 'Bout as usual. All the way up?"

"All the way. The boss must have pigeon blood, he likes it so high."

He gave the elevator operator a cheerful grin as they creaked to the top floor.

"You off duty at four as usual, Pop?"

The old man nodded. "If you ain't through by then, you walk down," he warned. "But you never are, are you, Mr. Waters?"

"Not while the boss is watching. But it's easier to walk down than up. Take care of yourself, Pop."

There were two doors in the hall, and one bore flaking lettering across its ground glass surface. But when the elevator sank out of sight Erskine unlocked the plain metal one leading to the roof. They mounted a·half flight of stairs to the open air. Before them was the canyon of the alley. Erskine lifted a board to the parapet, swinging it out until the other end rested on the warehouse roof.

"If heights bother you," he told Blake, just don't look down."

Once across, they descended a stair into a dusty corridor. There Erskine stopped, spread both hands flat against the wall, and under his pressure a panel moved, letting them through into one of the bedrooms of the hidden suite.

"Did you get it?" Hoyt stood in the doorway.

"Got it—*and* a lead. Beneirs, the owner, bought it from Geoffrey Lake, estate attorney. I put J.C. on to him."

"What's this about an attorney?" Kittson called from beyond.

Erskine made his report.

"Suppose he is really ill? Or could it be a stall?" Hoyt wondered.

"Pranj knows that we're here. But I'm inclined to think he sold that Ming-Hawn piece before he discovered that. He must need cash and need it badly; so I want to know a lot more about this Lake—especially about Lake's contacts, any visitor he's had since he went into the hospital." Kittson swayed back in his chair to study the ceiling. "Mr. Lake is ill. It is the proper time for Mr. Lake's dear friends to be thoughtful."

Hoyt got up. "Fruit, flowers, or the bonded stuff routine?"

"Flowers suggest the feminine touch. We don't know enough to venture that. Fruit is nicely middle of the road. A medium sized offering and you might put Mr. Beneir's card in it."

"What about moving? Are we going now?" Erskine asked as Hoyt went out.

"Sooner or later. Wait 'til Jas has checked the other

place. No use settling in there only to discover there are watchers about. We have some advantages including unlimited funds. And the type of henchmen Pranj has to enlist demand the pay on time. If he's taken to selling other level loot, it proves that the Hundred were able to seal off his resources back home."

The phone rang. Kittson listened. "Good enough. The usual fee will be mailed to you." He hung up.

"J.C. on Lake. He's middle-aged; from a family who have run the same law firm for four generations, conservative; most of the business is handling estates and trusts; a bachelor, nearest relative is a sister in Miami; had an operation two weeks ago; no direct contact with Pranj's men."

"Kmoat can be very convincing," Erskine pointed out.

"We'll let Hoyt learn what he can at the hospital. I want to know if Lake is shielded. And I have a feeling that from now on we may have to move fast."

He was interrupted by the buzzer, and then Saxton came in. He shed a conservative homburg and a well cut tweed top coat before he sat down.

"Everything is in order for the move. But our alley here is under observation. I had to use the roof route."

"Who's in the alley?" Erskine wanted to know.

"A muscular person we last saw supporting one of the walls of the Crystal Bird with his shoulders. He's one of their strong-arm boys. Do you know," Saxton took a cigar case from his pocket and made a careful selection from its contents, "the cleverest move for Pranj to make at present would be to involve us in some disagreeable incident which would focus upon our activities the attention of the local law? That would gain him time and force us to temporarily withdraw from this level."

To Blake's surprise he discovered that all three were looking to him. Kittson spoke first.

"What charge would you select to make us trouble with your police?"

"Considering your semi-secret set-up here," he answered slowly, "they might say gambling—or drugs. Either would get you raided. And a hint to a Syndicate contact that you were operating some new racket in a closed territory would bring them down on you too."

Saxton pursed his lips in a silent tut-tut. "In other words he could make us plenty of trouble now that he has run us to earth. I would say move and at once!"

Kittson nodded. "All right." He took a small map out of a drawer. "The Crystal Bird is located in the basement of that converted brownstone. Some apartments over it, aren't there?"

"Three, two occupied by members of the club staff," Erskine supplied.

"TV antenna on the roof?"

"At least one."

"Then we'll do the repair act."

"When?" Saxton wanted to know.

"Now. Send a messager through to clean out this place."

"Can't we eat first?" Saxton sounded plaintive and Kittson agreed after a short hesitation. They were gathered about the table when Hoyt returned.

"Boy friend in the alley and another keeping his eye on the sky route," he announced, "or is all this stale news?"

"Lake?"

"Well, he hasn't a shield. But I didn't get to see him. His sister is due in from Miami on the four o'clock plane—"

Kittson looked at Erskine. "A pleasant encounter between one lady and another out at the airport might lead to bigger things," he mused in a mild voice.

The slight man sipped his coffee slowly. "The things I

do for the Service! For this job I shall put in for the Star and Cross Bars."

Kittson's smile was ironic. " 'It is necessary at all time'," he was plainly quoting, " 'to select the agent to fit the job, and not the job to fit the agent.' "

"A beautiful bit of pass-the-buck if I ever heard one," Erskine remarked. "Meditation will supply me with a fitting retort. Also deeds, not barren words are the order of the day. I only hope that what I learn from this flying female is going to be worth going into skirts." He left from the table.

An hour later a fashionably dressed woman wearing a tailored suit with a mink clutch cape left the apartment accompanied by Saxton. And twenty minutes after that departure, Blake was a member of the second exodus. Neither Kittson nor the others had done any packing and it appeared that he himself was expected to abandon his belongings, a casual disregard for economics which bothered him.

Wearing the coveralls of repairmen, the three took the elevator to the basement. Hoyt's thick hair was now brown and there was an odd alteration in his jaw line, squaring it more, while two front teeth protruded a little in squirrel nakedness below his upper lip.

By the same mysterious means, Kittson's features had coarsened. The hawk sweep of his nose was thicker and displayed a reddish flush. The same craft made his eyes seem a little too close together, and he walked with a lumbering gait.

They did not go through the pawn shop but in the opposite direction, winding up through an air shaft court and a second door into a parking space. There was a panel truck, the sign on its side reading: "Randel Brothers, TV-Radio Repairs."

"You can drive?" Kittson asked Blake.

"Yes."

"Take the wheel; Hoyt'll direct you." With eel-sinuosity the tall man coiled up in the limited space behind.

"Straight on to the street and turn right."

Blake proceeded with caution down the narrow way.

"This is one bolt hole they didn't find," Hoyt commented as the truck edged into traffic.

But he was answered from the van. "Shielded mind not more than a half-block behind—"

Hoyt tried to look back. "We'll take the long way around just in case. They following, Mark?"

"Yes. I can't locate which car—too many on the street."

Blake wondered why he was not uneasy. Either the precognition which these others had insisted was his was not working on schedule, or they had nothing to fear.

"A green delivery truck, but it's turning off a block back" Kittson added to his report.

Hoyt's attention went to Blake. "How's the hunch working? Are we heading toward trouble?"

"Not as far as I can tell."

"That truck may be delivering another shift of stakeouts for duty, to watch an empty mousehole," Hoyt mused. "To be on the safe side, we'll lay a fancy trail. Turn left at the next corner, Walker, then straight on five blocks to the ferry."

"It's close to three o'clock." Kittson sounded a warning.

"Ferry takes about five minutes to cross. We can cut over the end of the freight yards and hit the highway at Pierce and Walnut. Make it back into town at the Franklin bridge. Use up about forty minutes, but if that doesn't foul up any tail, nothing will."

"Very well," Kittson sounded resigned.

On the ferry they changed drivers and by inspired mastery of his vehicle and a knowledge of routing, Hoyt brought them back into the city from another direction in five less than his forty minutes.

From the crowded business section they passed into a

district which had been fashionably residential fifty years or so earlier. Tall brownstones were built about an iron fenced park. But now many of the houses had fallen to the indignity of small grayish signs of "Rooms" in the lower windows and several had been converted into shops. Hoyt pulled up at the end of a block. The steep stairway leading down into the half-basement was covered with a curve of awning and a neon sign flashed on to notify the world that this was the Crystal Bird.

The thick winter dusk was gathering in and there was a hint of worse weather to come in the steady sifting of large snow flakes. As far as Blake could see, save for their truck, the street was clear of both cars and pedestrians. But after he had stopped the motor, Hoyt did not get out; he remained where he was as if listening. When he spoke, it was hardly above a whisper.

"Two shields in the club. But I think the house is clear."

"Yes," assented the unseen Kittson. Then he scrambled out of the back as Hoyt gave Blake his orders.

"Be ready to pull out in a hurry if we have to run."

Kittson came around and held out a comic book. "Stay in character but don't get too interested in the literature."

Blake slumped down in the seat, and over the edge of the comic watched the other two climb to the front door and be admitted by a drab woman.

More lights winked on through the dusk—dim ones in the "Rooms" houses, brighter ones in the shops. Now there were more people on the street. One man, his head bared in spite of the snow and rising wind, took the steps down to the entrance of the club with a speed suggesting he was late for an appointment. Blake wondered how it would be to reach out and read the thoughts of those passing.

Then came something he did understand—Danger! A smothering pillow of danger pressing down upon him.

He could taste it—feel it! Not since his encounter with the presence had Blake been so shaken. His fingers curled about the wheel and he forced himself to look about to try and discover the source of the warning.

He could see nothing new in the house containing the Crystal Bird. The neon blazed, a light or two was visible in the windows above. From that point his gaze traveled slowly down the block, appraising each house: no people, no cars. Wait!

On the other side of the square a delivery truck had stopped before one of the shops—a green truck.

Hoyt had ordered him to stay at his post. But over there he was sure was the source of his warning. If he got out—walked only a foot or two. . . .

Only the building tension held him in the driver's seat. On impulse he started the motor. He looked back at the club. A tall shadow flitted around the side of the house making for him; a second followed the first. Then the one to the rear stopped beside a rubbish can, grabbed off the lid and groped in its depths, just as the first reached the truck and climbed into the van. Blake gunned the motor. The man by the can thrust something into the front of his jacket and joined them with a couple of running leaps. As Hoyt got in Blake gave the warning:

"Green truck—there on right—!"

Hoyt leaned out as they swept past. " 'Denise, Gowns'," he read aloud. "Pranj disguised as three yards of silk and a belt buckle. Perhaps—"

But Blake's attention was divided between his driving and the overwhelming sense of menace.

"Turn right!" Hoyt snapped.

Another street of old houses. Street lamps made wild white whirls as the snow fell through their beams.

"Left, here—"

He drove automatically by Hoyt's direction. There was no sound from the rear where Kittson had gone to cover.

A series of turns brought them out on an avenue bordering the large park which almost bisected the city.

"Get into the park and then let me have the wheel."

Blake eased through the growing rush of homeward bound traffic and brought the truck into the obscurity of tree and brush which made an effective screen against city lights; then he changed seats with Hoyt.

They went on, switching from wider ways to narrow ones until at last they came out on a cindered parking lot beside a white theater-restaurant closed for the season.

"All out!"

Blake hit the cinders in time to see Kittson slam the back door.

"Come on!" The agent turned away.

"Where?"

"We get out of the park at 114th street. You cross the avenue there and wait on the opposite corner for the 58 bus. Take that and get off at Mount Union, about a forty minute ride uptown. Walk down Mount Union to the first street—that's Patroon Place. Go to the service entrance of the third house—the one with the wall around the yard. Knock twice. Got that?"

"Yes."

They did not speak again during the walk out of the park. And once outside the other two left Blake without a goodbye, speedily lost in the crowd on the pavement.

He crossed the street and joined the group at the bus stop. Fifty-Eights were, he discovered, not too plentiful, and he had to squeeze into a jammed one. The massed buildings of the lower city gave way to private homes set in yards.

There was a drugstore on the corner of Mount Union, a brilliantly lighted super mart of its kind. But the block he was to walk was dark, the lamps far apart. One block down and Patroon Place. He counted houses.

Number three had a row of lighted windows. The gate

49

to the drive was open and recent tire marks slicked down the snow. Sound was muted here. As Blake stepped over the beginning of a drift to reach the back door the wind drove a flurry of flakes into his face. He rapped as instructed. The door opened and Erskine drew him into light and warmth.

CHAPTER FIVE

WARM, DRESSED once more in his own clothes which had appeared mysteriously in an upstairs bedroom, Blake came into a small room furnished with the heavy pieces of an earlier century. Hoyt sprawled in one of the massive chairs.

He was watching with doting care a very small black kitten absorb chopped raw meat, and when he noticed Blake's arrival he indicated his feline charge.

"Meet the Missus. She sure can tuck it away, can't she?"

The tip of the kitten's tail flicked as if in acknowledgment of the introduction, but she continued to chase scraps of beef with single-hearted devotion.

"Did you take her out of that ash can?"

Hoyt's smile vanished. "She was tied up in a sack and left to freeze."

The kitten, her center section ball round, sat down to make washing dabs with her paw. She paused to look up at Hoyt, her baby eyes blue circles. Then with a spring she landed on his knee, kneading his slacks with thumb-sized paws, singing a song of content.

"She's going to be a help." Hoyt drew a finger around the furry head, rubbing all the right spots behind ears and in the angle of her jaw. "This level doesn't realize the possibilities of its natural resources. Cats and dogs and some birds can be contacted mentally if you try. Yes, Missus here is going to be a help. The more since Pranj," his grin was no longer pleasant, "hates all her kind. I wouldn't be surprised that it was by his orders Missus found herself exiled today."

The kitten relaxed in slumber and a drowsy feeling of well-being enveloped the room.

When Blake awoke in the morning, it was to the soft hiss of snow against the window pane. Outside drifts ridged high. Thursday; Blake counted off the days since this wild adventure had begun. It seemed longer.

The garage was open. Down a path shoveled from the house, two foreshortened figures, whom he was sure were Erskine and Saxton, went to get into the car and drive off.

Blake did not hurry. Who were the owners of this house, he speculated, as he went downstairs. There were two servants, a cook and a maid, who kept to themselves. Who had welcomed the agents here, and why?

Kittson was alone in the small dining room watching the snow swirl outside the pane. And the kitten sat on the sill, making dabs at the glass, as absorbed as its human companion. The radio had been turned on and the news-caster was announcing that the snow level was rising, that the city was fighting to keep the main streets clear. There followed some ominous comparisons to the big blizzard of five years back and the two-day tie-up of services which had ensued.

"It's getting worse," Blake ventured.

Kittson only grunted and the other realized then that the agent was in one of his trances of concentration. Were each one of these strangers in themselves receiving sets tuned in on message lengths they alone could pick out of the air?

Hoyt came in, his shoulders still powdered with snow. "It's almost as bad as glue," he informed them as he picked up the kitten. "Out this far they've given up trying to keep the side streets clean."

"If we're tied down by the weather," Kittson moved restlessly from window to chair and back again, "so is Pranj."

Hoyt shrugged and sat down, turning his attention to the kitten. If he had not witnessed what followed Blake would not have believed it. He had always heard that cats could not be trained to do tricks, that their innate independence kept them from obeying any will but their own. But in some manner the big man established contact with the minute bundle of black fur. Round kitten eyes stared into Hoyt's and the tiny feet moved, the small body climbed or ran, or little jaws closed upon a scrap of paper and carried it the length of the room to drop into a waiting hand. But kittens tire, and after a few moments Hoyt allowed his pupil rest.

It was mid-afternoon when Blake decided to go out. Both of his companions were in the peculiar trance state, perhaps they were in contact with action elsewhere. He was not only restless but in some way resentful, feeling as if he had been deliberately shut out.

The cook was standing by the back door. "Do you think you could get as far as the drugstore?" she asked abruptly. "Agnes has one of her headaches and will be good for nothing the rest of the day if she doesn't get her drops. The silly girl waited too long to have her prescription filled." She had a paper in her hand.

"I'll be glad to get it," he plunged out into one of the whirls of wind driven snow.

There was a holiday mood inside the store. Highway workers were gathered there drinking coffee, exchanging good and bad news with such customers as had fought their way in. Blake listened as he waited for the prescription to be filled. This was real—the way life was. The

52

fantastic world he had inhabited for the past three days was a dream.

How could one believe in other level worlds, in criminals hopping from one to the next, in psi men who could turn life upside down and shake it while you watched them? If he had any sense he would walk out now— away from the house on Patroon Place, out of the reach of Kittson. He could do it if he was not again nagged by the thought that it would do no good, that escape from those forces was impossible. Real world, dream, he was trapped in this.

But he was still rebellious, as he had been since waking that morning. He suspected that he was as much a tool in his way as the kitten Hoyt now trained. They would use or lay him aside as they thought expedient. It was a parent-child relationship and it aroused antagonism.

Was that resentment recognized and fed by something outside himself? Had he during those hours been deliberately prepared for what was to happen? Afterwards Blake sometimes believed that he had been so conditioned for the kill.

Outside the grayness of the afternoon had deepened into a premature night. Blake stamped off clinging snow between strides. Then he saw that other figure ahead. There was no mistaking, as he thought, the slim outline, the quick walk—Erskine.

A car came slowly along the cleared way. And with it a twist of apprehension hit Blake. Danger—danger for Erskine in some way. Blake shouted, plunging on. But the other, bending against the push of the wind, neither saw nor heard.

The car pulled up beside him, two dark forms dropped from it and went at Erskine in a rush. Blake's feet struck a slick patch of ice. He fought for balance, but at that moment a bolt of mental pain blasted him into utter blackness.

There was a throbbing ache beating in his head. Blake tried to remember what had happened. He was gagged, his mouth filled with cloth, tape across his lips. It was dark and his hands and feet were tied. When he jerked in his bonds he learned that the man or men who had put those on knew their business. He tried to roll over and discovered that he was inside a container, his knees cramped up against his chest.

Erskine! Had the other been taken prisoner, too? For all their powers the psi men had their limitations. Kittson had been unable to escape from the shielded thug in the Shelbourne. Blake wished though that he had one of the others' powers. If he could only communicate now with Erskine! He was still aware of his own private warning system, but he had met its prod so often lately that he was familiar with such uneasiness.

He was not dead so the kidnappers must have a use for him. How had they managed to get on the trail so quickly? Or had they been after Erskine and collected him as additional bonus? How long would it be before Kittson and Hoyt would discover and come to the rescue? (That they would not make any move on his behalf never occured to Blake.) Could their mysterious "Listening" inform them of this disaster?

No use asking himself questions to which he had no answers. It was more profitable to concentrate on what *he* could do . . . which was nothing at present.

Blake had no way of telling how long that trip lasted, but he felt the jerk of their stop. There were low voices. The box which held him was propelled forward and fell, jarring him painfully.

Warmth now and more voices. Something else. He caught a trace of perfume. At last a bump deposited the box on the floor and feet retreated. Warmth. Perfume. Blake strove to fit pieces together. The green van—the dress shop across from the Crystal Bird?

His cramped limbs were numb, he could do no more than move his head from side to side. There was a crack of light and from time to time he could hear muffled conversation.

Whe they did let him out he awould be a sitting duck, too numb with cramp to put up any resistance. But— Pranj was psi. And anyone raised in an environment where psi powers were the norm would depend upon those powers consciously and unconsciously, considering those who did not have them inferiors.

Blake had sensed a trace of this same attitude in the agents, although they had been conditioned to live as ordinary citizens of non-psi worlds. In the process of training they had lost their conscious superiority. But Pranj would have no reason to conceal his talents. Would not his dependence upon them blind him, lead him to under-value opponents except those from his own world?

In spite of his aching head, Blake forced himself to study the situation with what calmness he could muster. What did he have: a latent psi power of precognition of dangers and a strong mental shield. Very small advantages to set against Pranj's arsenal of invisible weapons. But the shield—it had held during his first encounter with the outlaw. Suppose such an attack would be leveled at him once more? Could he build on that barrier a false set of memories to be read by the enemy?

His body might be immobile but his mind raced, exploring that possibility. If he only knew more! Could he make Pranj believe that he was only an innocent bystander? With a few alterations he might tell the truth and it would bear that out.

What if he still believed that the agents were from the F.B.I. tracing a normal criminal of this world? The story would fit his actions and might satisfy Pranj into believing he was relatively harmless.

Without more than a vague idea of what he was trying

to accomplish Blake set to work. He recalled the details of his life back home—that he had come to attend classes at Havers. That was true—it could be checked. In his hotel room he had been startled by a sound, he made himself remember that sound. He helped Kittson to escape the thug. Kittson had shown him identification. They had made him join them. Ruthlessly he tried to overlay true memories with false. The visit to Beneirs, the assault on Tuesday, the story the agents had told him; he must forget those. And as he fought that strange battle in his own mind Blake was surprised. It was almost as if his efforts, crude as they were, awakened new skills, new and keener insights.

The light outside flashed off. For a moment Blake's preoccupation was broken by a wave of real panic. Was he going to be just left here? It was difficult to breathe, the cramp was crippling. Could he stand hours of such confinement?

That touch of hysteria was frightening until the new part of his mind, the section which observed and evaluated, saw how it could be put to use. To be afraid was the correct reaction. And fright in a way was telepathic, might be picked up by the enemy. Fear would add to his protecting cloak.

Blake had come a very long way since he had been taken prisoner, made a journey down a path he had not even known existed before. Shock was stimulating growth and he was no longer the same Blake Walker who had been taken captive on a snow-drifted street. He never would be again.

The light went on again; there was the heavy tread of feet. A cover was ripped off and he blinked up into brightness before he was sprawled out helpless on the floor. A kick twisted him around and he stared up at two men. Neither of these, even disguised, could be Pranj. Swiftly Blake thought bewilderment and fear.

"Yeh, he's one of them all right. And he's awake."

"Told you he was." The smaller man spat out a chewed matchstick. "What yuh gonna do with him?"

"Take 'im to th' boss. Git them ropes off his legs. We ain't gonna lug him."

The smaller man produced a switch blade and sawed at the cords about Blake's ankles. When he saw that the captive was watching him, he displayed rotting teeth in a grin and stabbed threateningly. Blake allowed himself to flinch and both men laughed.

"You be good, sonny boy, or Kratz'll cut more'n ropes."

"Sure thing," the other replied. "Me—I'm good with the sticker. Can carve you either neat or messy. Don't ask for it—see!"

Blake was dragged to his feet and slammed against the wall with a grip which kept him pinned in that position. The numbness in his legs gave way to the torture of returning circulation. As he was enduring this, a third man came in, a curious twist of his upper lip in a cruel dark face showing the points of two fang teeth.

"Take him over the lower way." One glance disposed of Blake.

"Sure, Scappa."

Between his captors Blake was hurried along in the wake of Scappa, down a dark hall and a flight of stairs. There was a well opening in the floor and Scappa descended into this followed by Kratz. Then Blake was lifted and dropped casually. He nearly blacked out with the force of his landing, but he was not allowed to lie in peace. The big man came down, picked him up, and bore him on.

Through an opening in the wall they came into a second cellar. Blake was placed on a chair, jammed against it so that his bound arms were crushed and a muffled grunt of pain forced out of him. The big man looped a strand of rope about him, anchoring him firmly to the seat.

Scappa jerked a thumb at his henchmen. "Get out!"

To Blake it appeared that the other two were only too glad to mount the rough wooden stairs and vanish through a trapdoor. Scappa, once they had gone, spread a handkerchief on a step and seated himself, lighting a cigarette. He had the air of one waiting for a curtain to go up on an eagerly anticipated theatrical performance.

When the assault came it was not the stabbing probe Blake had met before, but slow, inexorable pressure—a pressure which warned that this time the enemy meant to be the victor.

Blake held his thoughts to the selected memories he had prepared. It was easy to allow self pity to creep in also. Why should he be dragged into this battle. Slowly, under the prodding of the other, he revealed the meeting with Kittson and what had happened afterwards.

He no longer saw the cellar nor Scappa lounging there. In an odd way his sight was turned inward. Even his fear must be carefully nourished, but it must not reach deep enough to endanger the wall of his edited recollections. The invader must not realize that there *was* a wall!

Blake had no way of knowing whether he was standing up to the test or failing. The probes were sharper, deeper, as if the mind launching them was growing impatient. Wearily Blake held to his story and the weird interrogation continued in utter silence.

Then the mind touch of the other withdrew. Blake shuddered. Again he was left with the sense of defilement, violation. But he had also a spark of hope. The barrier had not been assailed with the strength he had feared. Did that mean that Pranj had accepted him for the innocent, normal world dupe of the agents? He was aroused by a slap which rocked his head. Scappa's features set in a sadistic mask flickered through a red haze.

"Come and get this punk!"

The big man clattered down the rickety stairs. Kratz followed.

"So what do we do with him?" the knife man wanted to know.

"Whatta yuh think? Unload him back with the gunsel. Then we can forget about him."

"Sure." The big man fumbled with the rope. "Big Boss git what he wanted?"

Scappa's grin faded. "Big mouths talk too much. Git him outta here!"

"Sure, sure!" the big man was instantly placating.

He propelled Blake through the opening in the wall. Halfway along the tunnel he stopped and Kratz shone a circle of light on a metal door. Drawing bolts he opened the portal just wide enough for them to boot Blake inside.

"Ask the gunsel to untie yuh, punk!"

Blake tripped, to slide along the floor, his face saved from a skinning only by the tape which held his gag in place. When he was able to twist his head around, the door had closed.

The dark and silence combined into a crushing weight. Perhaps he could inch his way to the wall and struggle up with his back against it. But now he was too tired to try. The chill from the pavement crept up his sweat bathed skin.

"In with the gunsel." He had been deposited in some private burial place. They had not retied his ankles, but his arms were a dead weight. Get up—move! But he was so tired; he ached with weariness.

Blake froze. There had been a sound out of the darkness. It came again from the other side of the unseen chamber. The gunsel. Blake controlled that thought. Something was moving now.

"Who's . . . who's there?"

Blake chewed on the gag which prevented him answering that hollow ring of voice.

"Why—why don't you answer me?" There was fear in that. "Answer me! Answer—!"

Movement again—toward him.

Erskine? Instantly Blake repudiated that. No matter what the ordeal he could not imagine Erskine's voice holding that note. He heard footsteps broken by pauses. Then a foot caught under his knee. With a scream the other tumbled across Blake, driving most of the breath out of him with the impact of their bodies. There was a flick of light, followed by an exclamation. Fingers explored his face, pulling at the tape.

With a cruelty which might be born of terror, the other ripped that away. The cloth was pulled out of his mouth and he was able to move his tongue. He wanted water more than anything he had ever desired in his life.

"Who are you?" demanded his companion querulously. "Why did they put you in here?"

"To get rid of me," Blake whispered huskily. "Can you untie my arms?"

He was unceremoniously turned on his face. His arms rolled, dead weights to his side, and he asked a question of his own.

"How long have you been here?"

"I don't know," the note of hysteria was stronger. "I was knocked out—woke up here. But . . ." Fingers dug into Blake's shoulder, pulling him up, "there may be another way out. They said something—"

With the assistance of the other Blake won to his feet.

"We go along the wall," he was informed. "There are only five matches left. And in the middle's a big hole."

The grip on Blake's shoulder urged him on that strange journey.

"You said 'another way out'?" he prompted.

"They said, earlier, before they threw me in. Something

funny about it—they laughed—kinda nasty. But anything's better than this!"

"Take it slow," he admonished a second later.

How long that inch by inch progress continued Blake could not have told. But he was sure that the chamber was a large one. Then that other spoke again with a trace of excitement.

"This is what I found jus' before they dumped you in. Step up!"

Blake's shin scraped against a rise about a foot above the pavement. He went down on one knee and explored the surface by touch. It was slick, almost greasy smooth. Metal? He stepped up on it.

"I found something stickin' out at this end; it feels like a crowbar. If we could twist it off then we'd have a go at the wall over on the other side. Some of the stones are loose there. But yuh gotta help me git this lever loose first."

Blake was tense. Through every nerve and muscle the warning shrilled.

"Don't—!"

He got out only that one word before he was thrown from his feet as the surface beneath him shuddered. A faint greenish glow gathered and he saw that he shared a small platform with another dark figure whose hands clasped a lever protruding from the surface under them.

CHAPTER SIX

THE RADIANCE was accompanied by sensation: wrenching, twisting, wringing which might be inside Blake, or actually heaving the raft on which they crouched. It seemed to him that this small square was the only safe refuge in a world gone suddenly mad.

Now that his eyes had adjusted to the light, dim as it

was, Blake could see walls—if they were walls—billowing like smoke beyond. The green glow was about them on four sides and beyond that was utter chaos.

Other lights flickered, blazed, and were erased by patches of dark, all the blacker in contrast. Once a cone of cold blue, somehow deadly, roofed them in for a space. Blake caught glimpses of other things, and he dared not believe them real. Strange vehicles flashed by and several times the platform was in open country— once a countryside where a war was in progress, judging by the flares of red, the roars and concussions which rocked the raft and deafened the two clinging to it.

The other whimpered in fear, burying his head, but his hands did not release their hold on the lever. Blake wavered to him. That bar must control this impossible journey. If they were ever to stop, his companion must let go. Under him the carrier vibrated with a life of its own, and always outside the green bubble weird scenes developed and broke. Blake crawled to the other, pulled at his arm. But the grip with which the frightened man clung to the simple control was so frozen that Blake could not break it. Finally he had to bend the other's fingers loose one by one.

As the hands dropped, the lever snapped up. There was a whirling, a sickening swing. Blake slumped, bumping his head as the flitting shadows outside the green solidified.

"Wake up! Wake up!" Fingers raked painfully across his skinned face.

"What—?"

There was a real light on, a steady glow, softer than that of the electricity he knew. And he could see the man who was bending over him. A small man, thin to the point of emaciation, with an unruly lock of dull brown hair flopping down to his wide, wild eyes. Hands jerked at Blake, trying to pull him up.

"Wake up, damn you!" There were tiny white flakes of foam at the corners of the other's mouth. "Where are we—tell me, where are we?" His voice shrilled to a half-scream.

Blake levered himself up and looked around. They were still on the metal platform but it was apparent that they were not in the underground prison to which Scappa had consigned them. This was a large room and the floor was paved with blocks of a rust-red, the same shade tiling the walls. There were no lighting fixtures he could see, the glow appeared to diffuse from the ceiling. Long bench tables ran around three of the sides, tables covered with a multitude of objects Blake associated with a laboratory.

Except for the two on the carrier the room was empty, but a flight of stairs led up into unknown regions. Blake edged toward the rim of the platform, eluding the grab the other made for him.

"Don't go!"

"Look here," Blake turned on him, "as long as you don't fool around with that lever we're staying here. But I want to know where we are."

Level travel was the only logical—the only sane—explanation of what had happened to them. And when the other looked at the control stick as if it were a flame-thrower pointed at him, Blake thought that he could be trusted not to touch it again.

Blake dropped his feet to the floor of that strange laboratory. He had half-expected that act to break the illusion—that everything would vanish when he tried to prove its reality. He stood up and moved a full step away. Nothing happened. It was solid under foot as the streets of the city where he had walked earlier. The faint plop-plop which had registered for the past moment or two proved to be the drip of water from a pipe running into a basin.

Water! Blake lurched across, catching at the table to regain his balance, to hold his hand under the leaky tap. Liquid ran over his dirty palm, trickled between his fingers. There was a row of buttons in the wall above the pipe. Made reckless by his thirst, he pushed the outer one on the right. The drip became a warm stream.

On the edge of the basin was a small cup, clean and dry. Blake filled it to the brim, gulping the tepid water. His thirst satisfied, he washed the grime from his puffed and swollen hands, allowing the water to run refreshingly over the deep purple gouges about his wrists before he splashed it over his face, where it stung in the scraped skin of his mouth and cheeks.

"Where are we?"

Blake looked around. The man had moved to the edge of the carrier and was staring about, curiosity plainly battling his fear. He was younger than Blake had first judged him, perhaps not beyond his own years, and his clothing consisted of a ragged pullover and a pair of dirt streaked corduroy pants. His brown hair needed clipping and his thin hands were never still, either pulling at his clothing or brushing that lock of hair out of his eyes and rubbing his chin.

"You know as much about it as I do," Blake countered.

The fellow did not look formidable, not that he would improve upon closer acquaintance either. But because they had made that queer journey together they were now united with an invisible, if uneasy bond.

"I'm Lefty Conners," the other introduced himself abruptly. "I'm a runner for Big John Torforta." He watched Blake narrowly as if trying to measure the effect of that announcement.

"Blake Walker, I was kidnapped by Scappa."

Lefty shivered. "He got me, too. Said I was workin' in his territory. That big goon of his put me to sleep and then I woke up in that cellar. Who you workin' for?"

"Nobody. I was with some FBI men and I think Scappa wanted to find out what I knew about them."

"Feds, yet! Whatta yuh know!" Lefty's interest was colored by awe. "Scappa's got th' Feds after him! Big John'll give a bill to hear that. But—" he glanced around and remembered," we gotta get outta here first. Only where's 'here'?"

"We came when you pulled the control on that," Blake indicated the carrier.

"I couldn't!" protested Lefty vehemently. "I tell you I walked all around that place we were stuck in—all around. And there wasn't nothin' like this—nothin' at all!"

"What's your explanation then?" Blake silenced the other effectively. His own version of what had happened to them was one he had no intention of voicing as yet. He had been in the hands of Pranj's dupes—and this was, without doubt, Pranj's means of traveling to other time levels. It looked as if someone had imprisoned them in the "contact" point on his world and Lefty's meddling had wafted them through a whole series of successor levels, which would account for the strange things Blake had sighted.

But how much of this dared he pass along to his new comrade-in-misfortune? Suppose by some miracle they could return to their own world? Then all that he told Lefty would cancel out his claim of ignorance. He decided to keep his mouth shut at least for the present.

"How about that hole in the floor you mentioned?"

Lefty, clearly startled, looked up at the ceiling. "You mean this here's some kind of an elevator, and we came down?"

Weak as that was Blake took it. "Your guess is as good as mine. At least we're out of that cellar."

Lefty brightened. "We sure are. And there ain't none of those goons hangin' 'round neither. What you say we have a look-see up them stairs? Geeze, jus' let me outta here and Big John'll pay plenty for an earful about this. Whatta silly lookin' joint this is. Whatta yuh suppose they do in here?" His nervousness was fading fast as his interest in his new surroundings grew.

"I'd say this was a laboratory."

"Like where they make atom bombs? Geeze—is that why the Feds are after Scappa? Maybe we'd better make tracks outta here but fast!"

Blake wanted to explore, he agreed with Lefty that far. But should they leave the vicinity of the carrier, their one link with their home world? He hesitated as Lefty, his self-confidence increasing with every stride, started toward the stairs.

"Get a move on, can't yuh?" the impatient whisper floated down as Blake followed, still reluctant.

He climbed into a short hall from which another stairway led up a second flight, and a half open door offered an invitation. Lefty was half crouched by the latter post of observation.

"It's some kinda store." But he did not appear too sure of his identification.

Shelves lined the walls beyond, crowded with small boxes and jars. The light was subdued and did not extend clear to the front of the room. Blake ventured in.

More shelves, save for where the door broke the pattern. There were no counters but a series of small tables with stools filled the main part of the open space. It might be a restaurant or cafe.

Blake tiptoed across to the front. There was another, wider door, perhaps giving on the street. His hand, resting on its surface, felt movement and he pushed aside a small panel. Yes—a street outside!

Snow lay in ragged, dirty patches, tinted blue by the rays of curious lamps fixed irregularly to the walls of neighboring buildings. He could see no tall structures and the street was narrow. Distinctly this was not the city he knew.

"Get away from there! Lefty's hand clawed at his shoulder. "Want some cop to see us? We could get picked up for a break-and-enter job jus' bein' here!"

Blake closed the panel. Lefty was right; he had no desire to attract attention. But he had to learn where they were. This must be played slow and easy, without Lefty catching on for as long as possible.

If he could find a newspaper or its equivalent—some clue. Blake turned to the nearest shelves and picked up one of the containers, looking for a label. The pot was earthernware, beautifully molded, the cone top peaked into a knob. And the knob was a small head. Blake brought it into the light.

A head, right enough, but the head of nothing which had ever lived on any earth he could imagine—a hideous, grinning devil's head. Something like a gargoyle with a voodoo mask added. He put it back and explored farther.

There were no labels on the jars and they were tightly sealed. But there were variations in the head knobs which perhaps identified their contents to buyers. The horned and grinning one was lined up with ten identical fellows. But next to that regiment was a colony of long fanged, wolfish things, and beyond them a collection of a dozen or so he recognized almost with relief as owls, very realistically portrayed. A swift inventory showed demons of various sorts and a few more animals and birds.

"What's in them things?" Lefty did not venture to touch the jars, but paced along the shelves surveying them.

"No way of telling."

Why didn't Lefty question their surroundings—this building? Surely he was not so stupid that he could not see this was extraordinary.

"Say!" Lefty stopped short, "D'yuh know—I think this

is one of them ritzy beauty shops where rich broads get their stuff straight from Paris."

"Could be." But Blake doubted if any woman would care for a jar of cosmetics enhanced by some of the gargoyle visages he could spot.

"Well," Lefty reached the door, "we ain't gonna get out this way. I bet if we laid a finger on the front door we'd raise an alarm to bring half the precinct boys down on our necks. Those ritzy places ain't never push-overs. Let's case the rest of the joint."

He went back into the hall and started up the second flight of stairs. Blake would rather had returned to the carrier. That platform had brought them here and if they were ever to return, it must return them. Was now the time to tell Lefty the truth? But something inside him still urged caution.

The stair gave on a second hall, longer than the one below. Blake surmised that the shop occupied only a limited portion of the building. Spaced along the wall were five doors, but none were open and there were no visible knobs or latches. The faint light coming from a blue line which ran along the molding made that clear. Lefty inspected the first with open surprise.

"Where's the knob?" he asked.

"The door might push to one side." But Blake was in no hurry to test his own suggestion. The last thing in the world he wanted to do was to walk into the private quarters of some other-level native, and try to explain not only who he was but what he was doing there in the middle of the night. With a faint shiver he imagined what would happen in a reversed situation in his own world—a marooned time traveler forced to account for himself before an assembly of indignant householders and police.

But Lefty was troubled by no such worries. He pushed

at the nearest door, and when it resisted his efforts, went to the next and the next.

"What th'—!" As he reached the last door it did not wait for his touch but slid smoothly back into the wall.

A trap? Almost it had the appearance of one. Lefty made no move to enter the dark space beyond. Were they now expected? Blake wanted to sprint for the uncertain safety of the carrier. But Lefty still teetered in the doorway. Curiousity was battling his caution.

He crossed the threshold and let out a frightened squeak. Lights had flashed on. A photoelectric cell control? Blake was hazy about these things, but it could be. He looked over Lefty's shoulder into what was without doubt a sitting room. There were chairs, rugs, a table, ornaments on the walls. And the fact that there was a subtle difference about each one of those did not greatly concern him now. The main fact was that the room was empty and there was something in its perfect order which suggested that it had not been in use for some time. Heartened by this, Blake pushed past his awe-struck companion.

The carpet underfoot was very soft, so yielding that Blake thought it closer to fur than any fiber. The chairs were barrel shaped, made of a light gray wood, each cushioned with a pad of silky fur. There were no lamps, the light came from a slender tube running about the four sides of the room at the join of wall and ceiling. Squares of opaque substance probably masked windows. Between these and over the long, fur-covered lounge were a series of masks hung like pictures. They were strikingly life-like, though Blake did not believe that they were meant as portraits. The eyes were exaggerated, set with gleaming stones in a flat, almost menacing, stare. Blake, after a single glance at them, preferred no closer study. If they *were* portraits he had no inclination to meet the originals. There were cruel curves to the mouths, promises of strange and evil knowledge in the staring eyes.

Along the full length of one wall was a case holding books, books encased in the same gray wood as formed the furniture. To his left were two others doors, both open.

Lefty, seeing that Blake had come to no harm, now sidled farther in. He stared about him as if the oddness of the place made an impression.

"Geeze—" was his acceptance of what he saw. "Some joint!"

He drew a finger across the cushion of the nearest chair. "Whatta yuh know—fur! And why all them faces plastered up on th' wall? This guy must be a head-hunter!" He started to laugh at his own flight of imagination but the laughter died away as he took a second look at the masks.

"This sure is a screwy joint. I don't get it."

There was no sound from the other rooms. Surely if the apartment was inhabited they would have roused some-one. But the feeling that the suite was deserted persisted, and his own private warning system gave him no hint of danger.

Blake went into the next room. Again lights flashed as he crossed the threshold, and he saw he was in a bed-room. The bed was low and wide, built into a corner, bunk fashion. One of the soft carpets—this time pure white—covered the floor. And the bed was spread with an embroidered cover glowing with color, sparks of gem-light reflected from points in the pattern. A chest of ebony wood inlaid with a design of leaves in red and gold was against one wall and above it hung a silvery mirror.

Catching sight of his grimy, disreputable self in that mirror, Blake was more than ever glad he had not blundered in upon a native. But the room was empty and again he had the undefinable feeling that it had been so for days.

"Geeze—" Lefty paid his favorite tribute. "Class, real class! Big John's dump ain't like this. Real class!"

The artist in Blake longed to examine the jewel-sewn cover, and all the rest of the treasures, but there was no time; to linger was foolish. They must get back to the laboratory and make an effort with the carrier even if it meant a return to the cellar where Scappa had imprisoned them. Something in the very air here suggested that Scappa, as bad as he was, might not be the greatest peril one could encounter along the worlds-traveling route. The marks had shaken Blake more than he cared to admit even to himself.

"We better get back—" he was beginning.

"Back where?" Lefty wanted to know. "Sure; I know we gotta get outta here."

Whether Blake could have carried his point about return to the carrier he was never to know, for at that moment there was a subdued chime, the first sound they had yet heard.

On the wall by the hall door was a round plate, resembling a porthole in a ship's cabin. But this was no longer dull gray. Three flashes from it riveted their attention. Lefty, with a cry close to a scream, simply turned and ran blindly out into the hall as a pattern began to form on the disc.

Blake stood his ground. There were lines of script— totally unfamiliar. And yet he felt they were allied to something he had once seen—that somewhere he had glanced over pothooks not unlike them. He roused from his study just in time to see the hall door close, sealing him in and Lefty out. He jumped for it, but there was a sharp click and for all his pushing it remained sealed.

Daringly he hammered on its surface, calling upon Lefty to release the catch by stepping in front. But, if the little man was still in the hall, he made no move, and the door continued to withstand Blake's efforts.

By the time he accepted the fact that he was now a prisoner, the message plate had gone dead. And he was very sure he could not depend upon Lefty to free him. He had been all wrong in keeping the full meaning of their journey from the other. Lefty wanted to get out of the building. Suppose he did leave—he would be an object of suspicion to the first native of this level whom he met. And the farther Lefty strayed from the laboratory, the more certain was their capture.

CHAPTER SEVEN

It must be well into the early morning hours, Blake thought. He now might have only a short time left before someone appeared to open the shop below—before workers were in the laboratory. He must get free!

He discovered a second door into the hall from the bedroom, but it resisted his efforts. The third room proved to be a kitchen. The sight of the appliances there, strange as they were, triggered his hunger. For a moment he wondered about a search for food, but common sense warned against that.

There was only one possible exit—a window. Breaking two finger nails he managed to loosen the panel which closed it. Still between him and freedom was a clear surface. Glass? No. Under his touch it bulged. He labored to force the second barrier, then he breathed air tainted with the usual city smells and some exotic new ones.

Blake's luck continued to hold. Some five feet below a ledge ran along forming a stepping stone to the offset roof of a first story projection. If he could worm through the window. . . .

It was a tight fit and he had to shed his jacket before he could make it. Then he stood shivering on the ledge before jumping to the offset. The bluish street lamps were far away but he could see a little. Here were none of the towering skyscrapers he knew in his own city. Few of the buildings were more than four or five stories high.

He looked down into a pocket of dark which was either a court or a backyard. Once there he might be locked out of the building and be even farther from the carrier.

As he hesitated, Blake saw two orange-red globes move majestically through the night sky, swinging in a circle above the city. Aircraft of some type? He turned to follow their flight and saw another light flash up in the building he had just left.

At the far end a window was a bright square in the dark. In fact it was so bright that Blake believed it must be open. If he could get in. . . .

He pulled himself up on the ledge once more, advancing toward that gleam. Had Lefty managed to get into another room? Then he could help Blake in; and this time he would be told the truth so that they could retreat to the carrier.

But innate caution made his approach to that light a stealthy one. And after he glanced inside, Blake stiffened.

Lefty was there all right. But an altered Lefty, a Lefty at perfect ease in his surroundings, a Lefty who bore only a very superficial resemblance to the frightened crook who had shared Blake's escape from the underground room.

The nervousness, the stare, the twitch of the lips no longer contorted the thin face which was now set in lines of calm force. The untidy hair was slicked smoothly back from a high forehead and there was an odd smile pulling the slack lips into firmness. He lounged in one of the barrel chairs and between his fingers he rolled a brownish cigarette. Lefty waiting—for what? Lefty at home? Here?

Only—the right answer shook Blake—this was not Lefty, not the frightened creature to whom he had felt so superior these past hours. He had been assured that only Pranj knew of the level worlds. Which meant, though the weedy little man in there bore little likeness to the image he had been shown, this was Pranj! A Pranj so able to fit himself with a new character that no suspicion of disguise had troubled Blake.

Then—they had not landed in this world by chance. This was a level Pranj already knew, a world in which he had contacts and a base of operation, a world in which he could dispose of Blake at his leisure, after getting out of him all that he knew. And now the outlaw would believe that his victim was safely waiting his pleasure.

Blake's hands balled into fists. He might not be a match for the psi powered criminal now. But let him reach the carrier—if he could, before the other realized that he was no longer locked in that suite.

A sound from the street sent Blake a step or two farther along the ledge to investigate. There was an egg-shaped vehicle drawing to a stop. From a hatch in its top three men stepped to the pavement and entered a door. Blake hurried back to the window.

On the wall before Pranj, one of the vision plates lit up with a message. He arose to press a button in the frame under the disc. And a minute or so later the three men entered.

Blake studied them. They were all tall and their dress accented the fine muscular development of their bodies: tight breeches with soft boots laced to the knees, jerkin-jackets buckled from throat to belt. Two of them glittered with embroidery of gold and silver, and their buckles and belts were gemmed, as were the guards and hilts of the knives they wore. The third man, who had a short shoulder cape of bright scarlet, remained by the door, his attitude that of a servant.

They were all dark skinned and their hair had been shaved to two narrow strips running from forehead to nape, leaving wide bare spaces above the ears. There was an arrogance about the two who seated themselves without invitation, the assurance of those whose will had never been disputed from birth. If these were members of some native nobility, it was a virile and dominant caste.

Since they were settling themselves as if for a conference, there was no indication that Pranj would be troubled about Blake for a time. Now he should move.

But he would gain nothing by returning to the locked suite; this left the street door through which the visitors had entered. Blake dropped to the offset, sped across it. The street looked deserted; in any event this was his only chance.

He landed with a jar, which brought a grunt out of him. It was to be hoped that the three had been the only passengers in the queerly shaped car. No one hailed him as he sprinted to the door.

It was closed but under his push it began to glide into the wall. Hardly daring to believe in his luck he entered, and not too soon for it snapped shut, catching a fold of his jacket. He tore savagely at the garment with no result; it was wedged fast. For the second time he had to slip it off, but this time it remained behind, a tell-tale sign of his passing.

That clue would shorten his time of grace. Blake sped to the foot of the ascending stairs and listened. There was no sound from above. So encouraged, he hurried down the other flight. The laboratory was just as they had left it, the carrier in its center. Blake remembered that he

75

lacked a weapon. If he were to return to his own time and the care of Scappa, he wanted one.

Swiftly he made the rounds of the tables. Something which could double as a club if he could find nothing better. He was reaching for a small hammer when he saw another object, a dagger similar to those worn by the native noble men. The ten inch blade was razor sharp, the needle point a threat. He thrust it into his belt, but before he left he selected another piece of loot, a smaller edition of one of the demon-headed jars, which he crammed into the front of his flannel shirt with the vague idea of using it to identitify this base of Pranj's if and when he ever caught up with the agents again.

Blake scrambled up on the carrier and reached for the control. In this light he was able to see as well as feel a series of small notches along the bar. Using his thumb as a measure he was able to assure himself that its position when they landed here had been at the last of those nicks. Another must stand for the world from which Pranj had originally fled—that of the agents. To get there might be a good idea. The inhabitants of that level would require no explanations and they would be in sympathy with his quest. He need only report to the agents there. He counted the notches again: five—six— Would it be the top one, since this was the last.

A shout carried through the building, jerking him around. He pulled the lever—first notch it would be. But the control did not yield to his tug. He twisted it; and there was the pound of feet on the stair. A second cry with a note of triumph in it. They must have found his jacket!

Blake worked feverishly at the rod and then threw himself down to examine the shaft from which it projected. There was a catch there! And it held stubbornly.

A clatter of feet on the stair. Blake pried at the catch with the point of the dagger and someway touched a spring. It gave, and with both hands on the control, he looked up. They were strung out along the stair: the red cloaked men in the lead and Pranj in the back as if he were a commander who led his armies from headquarters well to the rear. But of them all, Blake was most conscious of the fury on the changed face of "Lefty."

The red cloaked man raised a tube, sighting along it as if he were aiming a rifle. Blake had no time to pick or choose. He simply thrust the control forward, but in that second a numbing blow struck his shoulder and his left arm dropped useless to his side.

Once again the humming, the rise of the green globe of light to encase the carrier. There was Pranj and the others, the three natives open-mouthed with astonishment, Pranj displaying the cold and deadly anger of one who has underestimated an opponent and so lost an important move. Was he exiling Pranj in this world? Blake speculated with a soaring sense of triumph.

Then the laboratory was gone and the stomach and nerve wracking journey through the light and dark began. Blake lay flat, his head pillowed on his good arm, his deadened left one along his body, content to rest and leave his escape to the machine he did not understand.

Lights. Dark, lights. Blue fog. Lights. Dark. The carrier no longer quivered under him. His voyage was ended, and he was in darkness. But with that, exhaustion conquered and Blake slept.

He awoke cold—cold and stiff. His eyes opened and he did not understand. There was a pallid light, a splotch of weak sunlight spotting his hand. Sun!

Stiffly, every muscle protesting, Blake raised himself on his right elbow. Moving his left shoulder sent a thrust of burning agony down his back and breast, tearing a little cry from his raw lips. And, when his head cleared, he stared about him in horror. He had thought himself free!

But this was not the underground room he had left

sometime the night before (was it only yesterday?). Time no longer had much meaning. He hunched together, supporting his left arm across his knees, gazing dully at what encircled him.

Walls of stone, rough hewn in mishapen blocks, but fitted together with an engineer's precision which left no cracks, spiralled dizzily upward. The carrier rested in the bottom of a dry well was his first confused thought.

But about six feet above there was a break in that wall through which the sun shown, promising a way out. Blake, a little light-headed, got to his feet. The carrier was not steady under him, rocking a little when he moved. It rested on a mass of blackened stuff, from which protruded the jagged and charred end of a beam. And now he noted that the walls about him bore traces of an old fire, fire which must have eaten out the heart of the structure—perhaps in the far distant past, because when he ventured to kick at the beam it powdered away to dust.

This was certainly not Scappa's cellar; nor was it, he was quite sure, the world from which Pranj had fled. Unless the outlaw had chosen to operate out of a ruin far from the main settlements of his race.

Moved by that thin hope, Blake paced about the circumference of the wall. His feet sank almost ankle deep in the charred debris, but, as far as he could see, there was no opening in the stone surface at this level. Any entrance must have been made from above. He eyed the break; it was surely wide enough to provide an exit. Whether he could make it with the use of only one hand was another matter.

Blake sat down once more on the carrier. His hunger was now a gnawing ache in his middle; he ran a dry tongue over dryer lips. He wanted food and water. Should he trust again to the blind chance of the carrier, hoping to land either in his own level, or that of the agents, or should he explore further here?

If Pranj had established bases along the line the carrier was geared to, he might find trouble awaiting him anywhere he dared to stop. And he remembered the agents' warnings concerning level worlds where even their trained investigators dared not venture—the radioactive worlds, and those where humanity had taken other and more desperate roads for survival.

It was quiet here and the ruins suggested that this might be a deserted and relatively peaceful pausing place. He could rest, collect his wits and do a little planning. But first—food—warmth—he shivered as a breeze licked down at him through the shattered wall.

Blake went to the wall. Somehow he made that climb, hitching his way up and over. But a weary time later, shaking with weakness, he stood on the ground looking dazedly around.

There was pavement under his feet, uncovered in places where the wind had scoured away the snow, which in other spots drifted about the bases of towers, the boles of stunted and wind carven trees, now barren of leaf. But that pavement was not any civilized street—instead it was a circle of flagstones with withered clumps of grass and winter-dried brown weeds pulling block apart from block. It was plain that no one had walked this way for a long time.

Blake went down on one knee, scooped up a handful of snow and licked it from numbed fingers. But his eyes swept from one tower to the next, from trees to wall of brush. No tracks of either man or animal patterned the snow. Except for the whistle of the wind playing hollowly across the broken towers there was no sound.

Painfully he dragged clumps of the withered grass free from the frozen soil, and then went farther afield for fallen branches, half rotten sticks. He would have to have

79

a fire—warmth. There was a book of matches in his pocket—he held a tiny flame to the withered grass twist. It seemed, Blake decided with a wry grin, that he was not altogether helpless in his Robinson Crusoe guise.

The blaze caught; the flames were warm on his half frozen body and blue hands. Blake became aware that some measure of feeling was returning to his left arm as the heat of the fire struck in. But whenever he tried to move it, pain streaked out from the point on his shoulder. He could see no blood, no sign of a bullet.

Clumsily he unfastened his upper shirt, the clothing underneath, trying to find the wound. Just below his collar bone was an angry red patch which resembled a burn. Well, there was nothing he could do about it now.

Instead, as he rebuttoned his clothing, he gave his surroundings a second and more intent study. The ruined towers, he could count at least ten within easy sighting, did not appear to be arranged in any consistent pattern of streets or a city such as he could recognize. And there were no other buildings except the tower form to be seen. Towers, which could only be entered from above, which did not even possess slitted windows. That suggested defense—a needed defense of the most serious kind. And yet that tower from which he had just climbed *had* been stormed, stormed and burned.

A people who had been so hard pressed by some enemy that they had lived in a constant state of siege—a people who must in the end have fallen victim to that same enemy a long time ago.

But the enemy? Had the invaders, or besiegers, having won their victory withdrawn, content with the total destruction of the conquered? He could see nothing to suggest that there had been any attempt to rebuild from the tower ruins.

Blake licked more snow from his hand. Something to eat. This place had gone back to the wild. Rabbits, birds, were everywhere. He had never hunted, and how efficient he would be with only one usuable hand he dared not guess. But he had fire and a knife. And if man had long vanished from this place not only should there be small animals prowling among the ruins, but they should also be unafraid and so the easier to bring down. He kicked at the frozen rubble and chose some stones which fitted into his hand. When a man knew how to pitch a baseball, he ought to be able to aim at a rabbit.

He fed the fire with a couple of large chunks likely to last for a while and plotted a path toward a more distant tower whose crown was broken into two parts rather like a pair of teeth gnawing at the morning sky. With that as his goal, and a keen eye for the spoor of game, Blake started off.

The weird sighing of the wind was disconcerting. Sometimes it raised to a scream as it forced across the empty throats of the towers and through gaps from which stones had fallen. Twice Blake sprang for cover, sure that the sound he had heard *had* come from some human throat. But he saw nothing.

He was heartened by the unmistakable tracks of a pigeon in snow, and then, at the foot of another tower, the paw mark of some small animal he was not woodsman enough to identify. But at that moment any animal meant only meat and he followed the trail.

It led straight to another tower where a large portion of the wall had collapsed. He caught a stale whiff which spelled den. But that did not interest him as much as something else.

Inside there had been another and more recent fall of masonry. And it had broken open an ancient storage place. Blake was deafened by the whirr of wings as pigeons and other birds beat out at his coming. Piles of grain had trickled from the stone coffer, offering such bait as he did not count on existing. He was sure the birds would return. Scooping up a fistful of the stuff, he chewed it as he flattened back into the protection of the remaining wall to wait.

He was right; the pigeons returned first, greedy for the treasure. Blake knotted small stones into the opposite corners of his handkerchief. There was a plump white bird right along a line of scattered grain. . . .

An hour later Blake made a rude toilet in the snow. Meat without salt, even when toasted to take the rawness out, was not the most appetizing dish in the world. And the dusty, gummy taste of the grain he had chewed still clung to his tongue. But he was no longer hungry. Not only that, but deep inside him he had a new satisfaction. He had been moved about by the agents in the game against Pranj. And in turn he had been fooled by the outlaw.

But he *had* escaped from Pranj. And here, without tools or any real knowledge, he had managed to achieve food and warmth. No thanks to anyone but himself. Some measure of confidence had returned to him.

What had finished off this city? War certainly. But what kind of war? Who had fought whom? Had the tower people been of his own kind—overwhelmed in their refuge by savages who had no wish to follow up their advantage? Had this been the last stronghold of civilization on this world?

Curiosity tugged at Blake. He wanted to explore—to learn. He reached mechanically for more wood and then paused. Why build up the fire? He ought to return to the carrier to try it again. . . .

He stiffened, so startled he did not remember the dagger in his belt. Above the wind screeched in rising fury. But Blake heard nothing, saw nothing but the thing which had crept up through the brush, its eyes reflecting the light of the flames.

82

CHAPTER EIGHT

THE DRAGON of Teutonic folk lore, the very personification of nightmare crouched there. It was about seven feet long, and jointed, a bulbous head stretched for a third of its length above its many-footed body. And the fire was reflected in glassy eyes, which were the only features in that noseless, mouthless face—if you could term it a face.

Blake retreated step by step as the thing crept as cautiously forward. He could not tell as yet whether it was attracted solely by the fire, or whether he was the bait. It moved, slow as its pace was, with a fluidity which suggested that its attack might be hard to counter.

His shoulders pressed against the stone of the tower wall, sending a thrill of pain shooting down his back and injured arm. And that red agony broke the spell. He drew his dagger as the creature half-crouched before the fire, staring with the same bemusement into the flames.

Blake drew a long breath. Each segment of that silver-gray length wore armor sheathing like a beetle's shell, and the thing twisted and turned upon itself with a worm's ease. So far, it had shown no interest in him, nor could he say that it was a danger. If it would remain where it was—enchanted by the fire—he might be able to run to the carrier and safety.

The round head of the creature turned; it gave the impression of listening intently. Blake, however, heard no sound except the ever present whistle of the wind. And then his warning sense went into action. It had not heralded the approach of the worm, but now. . . .

Too late for him with his crippled arm to climb the wall; the worm could pull him down. And the creature was moving around the edge of the fire. Under some of its feet, stones rolled and it slid to one side. A clang as of metal against stone sounded when the thing brushed a large block. Metal!

The worm flashed around the block as if the small mishap had angered it, and now it coiled before him, its head raised, the round red eyes regarding him without expression or life. They were like glass bulbs. . . .

Glass. . . .

Blake had been so intent upon the worm that he was not aware until now of the figure which had approached noiselessly from the same direction. Not until the stench, which cloaked it as a garment, brought his head up. A worm-dragon, and now—an ogre! Again he returned to the tales of his childhood for a description to fit.

Mats of filthy hair covered a skin which might remotely have been whiter than his own, but which was now so caked with ancient dirt that it had a dull gray cast. The thing was not wholly animal, though he wished that he could so classify it. Not quite an animal. For about its middle was a kind of kilt of untanned skins, rotting in tatters from the thong which served it as a belt. The creature crouched in what was probably a perpetual stoop, strings of hair half masking the vacant horror of its face. But the worst of all was that it was so plainly a female!

The worm made no move, nor did it turn to acknowledge the arrival of the other. It remained in position as if holding Blake at bay according to some order.

But the hag was content to hunch down by the fire. Until suddenly she raised her frowsy head and looked straight across the flames at Blake. Her eyes were no longer as vacant as those of her worm-hound, but feral, the eyes of a carnivorous hunter. The slack lips folded back from teeth which could not have budded in any strictly human jaw, fangs which would better serve a wolf or a mountain lion.

Ropy muscles moved under the scaled and warty skin

as almost lazily she raised hands ending in the hard and pointed talons of a beast.

"No!" Blake did not realize that he had voiced that protest until the word was echoed back to him from the hollow towers.

And, as if his cry had broken some last restraint, the hag opened her slavering mouth and howled a challenge. For the first time she arose to her full height and her stringy leanness gave such an impression of menacing strength and avid hunger that Blake tensed, ready to meet the rush which would bring her at his throat.

But the worm moved first. With a lithe uncoiling of its limber segments it reared up and forward. From somewhere under its belly shot tentacles which snapped about Blake with bruising force, pinning him to the rough stone of the wall. And the touch of those limbs burned! The thing *was* metal! There was no mistaking that—just as the red orbs now on a level with his own eyes were not natural organs of vision at all.

He was as helpless as he had been when bound and gagged in the hands of Scappa's goons. The worm—thing—machine made no move to crush him. It only held him, waiting for an order from the crone.

Again that creature voiced her howling challenge, or was it a summons to others of her kind? Blake shivered and then he struggled vainly against that hold—the only result unbearable pain from his shoulder. His whole being shrank from any physical contact with the hag, yet now she was shambling about the edge of the fire toward him.

There was another sound—a sharp snap. It could have been a stick breaking under an incautious foot. But it was not.

From the matted hair on the hag's breast a bright blue shaft protruded. Dancing, she uttered a series of eerie shrieks until blood frothed between her lips, then crumpled down, her hands and feet scrabbling on the ground in her last struggles.

The worm did not loosen its grip; it did not even turn its head to watch the death throes of its mistress—if that was the relationship between them. It merely stood its ground, locking Blake to the stone, the chill of its metal body icy.

Out of the same patch of brush which had masked the arrival of the worm came another, walking with the assured tread of one who is master of his environment and has little or nothing to fear from the world about him.

Eskimo? Blake's first confused thought identified the fur clothing, the parka-like upper garment. But the hood of that parka was flung back and who ever saw an Eskimo with the features of a South Seas Islander? Features embellished with tattooed patterns in dark blue, patterns suppling with graceful spirals and dots the beard lacking by nature.

The fur clad Polynesian halted a step or so away from the hag. He surveyed Blake with open curiosity, paying no attention to the worm. Then he stopped, selected a piece of rough stone, and came around the fire. The worm did not move, nor did it show any interest in the newcomer—it might now be a part of the tower.

With no concern the fur clad hunter brought his stone down to smash one of the red globes sprouting from the worm's head. Then with a speed which left Blake a little dizzy, he struck at the second organ. There was the tinkle of breaking crystal but still the worm did not move, made no defense against the attack.

The hunter put out his hand and jerked at one of the tentacles which imprisoned Blake. At first it clung, then it gave and the creature crashed to the ground, plainly out of commission. The hunter laughed and toed it with his fur boot before he went to pick up his weapon—a form of crossbow. He ground this between his feet as he turned to face the other. His bare hands were held up in the universal sign of peace—empty and palm out.

Shakily Blake hurried to copy that gesture. The stranger voiced a question in a liquid trill. Regretfully Blake shook his head.

"I do not understand," he answered slowly.

The other listened carefully, his mobile features registering surprise, as if a different language was the last thing he had expected to hear. But he did not show alarm. Instead he made an inquiring gesture to the fire, giving an exaggerated shiver. Blake stood away from the wall and tried to put all the good will he felt into a sweeping invitation to enjoy the heat.

It was accepted, the stranger squatting down to hold his hands to the blaze. Blake, still shaken, sat down on a block of stone. This Eskimo, or Hawaiian, or whatever he was, seemed disposed to be friendly. But would that friendliness continue if Blake tried to reach the carrier? And flattened against the wall, in the climb he would present a perfect target for the other's crossbow.

The man across the fire was working on his weapon, rubbing the string of the bow between thumb and forefinger. He smiled at Blake and spoke again as if the other could understand. Then he got to his feet in one graceful movement.

Before Blake could protest he began putting out the fire, smothering the flames with snow. When Blake shook his head, the hunter laughed and pointed to the worm and then to the warmth he was destroying, suggesting that the fire would draw such.

The worm was a machine. Blake was now sure of that. But any civilization which could produce so intricate a robot as that and then paired it with the beast-hag. . . . He could not fit the two into any sane companionship. Nor did the worm fit the civilization which had built the towers, at least from casual inspection it did not. And it certainly was not connected with the hunter or he would not have destroyed it so quickly. Thoroughly muddled, Blake longed to make a break for it—back to the carrier.

When the last spiral of smoke died, the hunter went to the crone, performing an act of such savagery that Blake, shuddering, retreated once more to the wall, trying to figure a way of winning over it while the other was engrossed in his butchery. For the hunter deliberately smashed the jaws of the hag, groping among the bloody splinters to bring out a couple of the animal fangs. He rubbed these clean in the snow with a business-like dispatch and then stored the trophies in a pouch swinging from the broad leather band that belted-in his parka.

With a grin, into which Blake was no longer so quick to read friendliness, he turned and beckoned the other to join him. Determinedly Blake shook his head. He had no doubt that the dagger was little or no protection against that crossbow. But neither was he going to be tamely led away from the carrier into a world which certainly had more than one lurking danger.

The smile faded from that elaborately tattooed face. The eyes narrowed. Good nature had been wiped from the tough mask of a fighting man who was and always had been top dog in his particular section of the earth. The crossbow came up, its sight on a line with Blake's chest.

And Blake could not forget that bright blue dart which had killed the crone, the unhurried and practical way the hunter had disposed of the worm—as if each act was an everyday occurance. Now Blake presented a good mark. Again the hunter perked his head in an order, his hands sure on his weapon.

The wind which had howled over their heads now carried snow with it: a powdering of small hard balls, and Blake shivered as it lashed through his clothing. With the fire out and the other impatient to move, with no common speech in which to explain or appeal, Blake realized the folly of resistance. If he antagonized the hunter it would only make his situation worse.

He moved, circling the snuffed out fire, avoiding the body of the hag. And the hunter fell in behind him, cradling the crossbow on his arm but leaving Blake in no doubt that he would use it should the other prove stubborn.

They forced a crackling path through the brush as the snow fall thickened. Blake tried to mark the trail, note the position of the towers within sight, locate any guide which would bring him back to the carrier if and when he managed to elude his captor. He had no longer any desire to explore here . . . Escape—even to Scappa—to a world where he could in a small way predict danger to come was better than this.

On the other side of the thicket they came upon a well-beaten trail worn a foot or more deeper than the surrounding ground, but so narrow they would have to travel it single file. The hunter motioned Blake to the north, waiting for him to step into that slot before he followed.

The path wound, purposelessly as far as Blake could see, about the bases of several of the towers, sloping downward. Here the wind was shut away by a stand of trees. A branch way curved from the track, running to a tower which was largely a tumbled heap of stone. Blake's nose wrinkled at the sour-sweetish stench issuing from that dark hole.

His captor gave a soft exclamation and Blake saw the other spit at that opening, loathing plain to read on his face. He had stopped, and now he fumbled with one hand at his belt, loosening a small box clipped there. He gave that to Blake with an order the other could not translate. But, since it must be connected with the box, he snapped up the lid.

The interior was lined with clay blackened and baked and a small coal winked red. Blake glanced up to find his companion making gestures—pulling up a handful of the withered grass. Apparently Blake was expected to build another fire—right there and now. The why he could not understand, but he gathered from the other that it was in some manner vitally important.

On an open space not far from the lair, he achieved a small blaze. The hunter moved no closer to the heat. Instead he was alert, watching, his attention for the mouth of the den. Plainly the blaze was intended as a lure—for what? Another worm—another non-human crone?

The wind died and they were caught in an odd pocket of quiet. Through that stillness Blake heard a clinking, the click of metal against stone. A worm! He looked about for some rocks. Now that the hunter had demonstrated the proper way to deal with the things he would be prepared.

But it was no seven foot monster of gleaming metal which crawled to their bait. A small glittering thing darted to the fire from the shadow of the den and then another and another!

Blake prepared for a dragon was faced by a handful of contipodes less than five inches long. Young! But that metal creature he had seen was manufactured. A robot; he was certain of that. It could not have reproduced its kind.

The hunter stalked forward and brought his heel crunchingly down on one of the glittering things, motioning Blake to join him in that act of righteous destruction. Blake struck with a stone and then picked up the smashed body. His blow had broken it open and he was right—inside was intricate machinery, too delicate and involved to study without time—it was truly a robot. One more mystery to be added to all the others this level offered.

His fur clad companion was searching about the edge of the fire, prying up loose stones, hunting for more of the small worms. But, save for four smashed bodies, the ground was bare. At last, with a grunt, he began to put out the fire.

With the satisfaction of one who has done his duty, he motioned Blake on once more when the blaze was out. The worn trail led away from the towers now and there were no more breaks in it, no more lairs of the metallic monsters and their sub-human mistresses.

They came out on a headland and Blake looked over an arm of the sea. It wore its gray winter guise and there was a rim of ice along the shore below. The path they followed so far now became a series of hand and footholds leading ladder-fashion to the beach. Painfully Blake made the descent, given no choice by his guard. He was able to use his left hand now, but the resulting pain brought cold dampness to his forehead and made him bite hard on his underlip.

On the beach, back against the cliff wall was the hunter's camp. A queer, blunt-bowed boat fashioned of skins drawn tightly over a frame of light metal and smeared with a thick and shiny substance, was drawn up on the sand well away from the reach of the waves. While a shallow indentation too shallow to be termed a cave, had been enlarged as a shelter by the addition of a projecting brush roof and walls making a snug lean-to cabin snug for one, cramped for two.

Hides were stretching on boards against the cliff and wraps of fur strips cut fine and then woven into blankets covered a bed of springy pine branches. There were strong smells from the raw pelts, and the wood smoke, but none of the filth born stench which had wafted from the tower lair.

Now that he had Blake in his own territory the hunter relaxed his watchfulness, stowing away his crossbow before stirring up the fire and preparing a meal. The appointments of the camp were a queer mixture of civilization and the primitive. For the fur blankets, intricately woven as they were, might belong to a forest dwelling barbarian. While a set of nested bowls, almost translucent as the finest china, yet of some incredibly tough substance, bowls which could safely be placed on hot rocks in the center of the fire without melting or cracking, were beyond any product Blake knew of in his own world.

The hunter shed his parka, as if to prove that he himself was a study in contrasts. For under the thick fur he wore a shirt of some silky material which molded itself to his powerful chest and shoulders almost as if painted on his skin. It was of a flaming scarlet with a pattern of dots and circles, such as formed the tattooing on his face.

Savory steam arose from the bowl over the fire and Blake swallowed. The musty grain and the half-burnt, half-raw scraps of pigeon he had downed earlier were very remote memories.

His host ladled stew into a small bowl and then produced a horn, carved and embellished with inlay, from which he drew the stopper to pour a small portion of its contents into a handleless cup he tendered to Blake with some ceremony.

Blake's hands were shaking so that he had to use both of them to raise that cup to his lips. He gulped a mouthful. First it was bland on his tongue; then it came awaking to warmth in his throat and then to fire in his middle—a fire from which a glow spread throughout his cold and starved body.

The hunter took back the cup, refilled it to the same mark and uttered a sentence before he tossed it off with a single draft. Then he drew a knife from his belt and fell to spearing chunks of meat and unidentified vegetables out of the stew. Blake pulled out his dagger and followed his example.

As his hunger was appeased and he was relaxing in the warmth of the small cabin he was troubled once again by the parodoxes of this level. Was this one of the bases set up by Pranj, or had chance—chance and the shot which had numbed Blake's arm—brought him into an unknown, unexplored world? And what historical event of the remote past had produced the fallen towers, the sub-human hags and their mechanical serpents—this fur clad islander?

Speculations had to be wild to cover all the points. He would like to show Saxton this level and ask for a logical explanation. Blake's eyelids seemed weighted. He leaned back against the side of the bed. The hunter had taken up one of the stretching pelts and was working over it. Blake's eyes closed in spite of his struggles and he fell asleep.

CHAPTER NINE

THE BOAT on the beach was marked by a mound of snow, and the white stuff had drifted high about the entrance to the cave-cabin. Blake pulled the hood of the parka, which had been flung over him while he slept, higher about his ears and wondered if this was the time to cut and run, if he could make the carrier before his host-guard caught up with him. The hunter had left some minutes earlier; Blake watched his exit from beneath lowered eyelids, trying to play the man deep in slumber.

But he was reluctant to face the storm without. He kept telling himself that in that whirling white curtain he would lose all track of landmarks, that he would quickly be lost and unable to find his way to the tower which held the carrier.

During the past hours he had tried to discover whether Pranj had visited this level. Though he was no nearer solving the mysteries of this world and he probably never would, he had established a limited communication with the hunter. The latter was named Pakahini; his true home lay to the westward across the arm of sea which lapped this island; he had come here to trap for the fur of a variety of animal numerous on this site but greatly prized in his own community. With pride he had displayed his catch: creamy white skins Blake could not identify. He had almost completed this particular trip, and was now gathering in his traps and bundling his take, preparatory to returning to his own people.

But to all Blake's halting inquiries concerning the hags and their worm-hounds he replied with shrugs so the other did not know if he was not making his questions clear, or whether the other refused to discuss the subject. Blake suspected the latter.

To his surprise the hunter had his own explanation for Blake's appearance, one to which he had only to agree, when the other stated it, to have it readily accepted. He was, in the other's belief, the victim of a shipwreck. And, Blake thought with a wry grin, that was one way of looking at his arrival by carrier. His alien speech and dress to Pakahini meant that he came from overseas, which argued that the hunter had met travelers from the East—or had heard of them—and so was able to accept that idea readily.

But Blake did not accept, in his turn, so easily the present plans of Pakahini. Both of them, he gathered from a long speech the other had made that morning, were to return in the boat to the town of his people. Blake's clothing had been fingered with appreciation, his belongings examined. Proof that he was from a highly civilized community was plain, and Pakahini wanted to display him to his tribe.

The hunter's own degree of culture was, Blake guessed, on the upward grade. His people were thirsty for new skills, for anything which would add to their advancement. They were not of the race which had built the towers. Pakahini had managed to give the impression that the towers were already old ruins when the first tribes of his race had penetrated into this section. And his people did not work in stone at all.

But all this, Blake told himself, was not solving his own problem. If he remained in this camp Pakahini would return. And eventually he would find himself in the boat out there, being paddled north to become a trophy for the hunter to show off in his village. Once off the island, the American might never be able to win back to it. He would have to move—and right now!

Blake raised his left arm as high as he could, flexing the fingers of that hand grimly in spite of the pain all movement brought. The stiffness was going, but he still did not dare to put much weight upon it. That climb to the trail above—he wondered if he could make it. The alternative was to walk along the shore and hope to discover an easier slope. With the danger of being lost by venturing too far from the trail at the top of the cliff.

He finally decided on the shore path. If he overtaxed his arm now, what of the climb into the tower? He might reach his goal only to be baffled in the last few feet!

Snow beat about him and he pulled the parka hood over his head. He tramped along so close to the cliff wall that his shoulder brushed now and again against the rock, his guide in the storm. One good thing about the snow: it would cover his trail speedily. If Pakahini was gone long enough, he could not track the runaway upon his return.

Already the hunter's camp was hidden, not only by the

storm but also by a turn in the cliff wall. Blake pushed on, glad that the wind was at his back. He had no way of measuring either time or distance but finally he found what he sought, a break in the walls, a staircase of rock ascending from a flat platform of stone running out into the waters of the bay. Some relic of the tower people he supposed.

The broken and crumbling steps were coated with ice where spray had frozen. He eyed them doubtfully and then solved the problem in his own fashion by seating himself on the nearest and then rising to the next— "bumping" up as in babyhood he had "bumped" himself down a more familiar stairway. It was an odd way to make the climb but the safest that he knew, and it put little strain on his shoulder.

Twice he skidded and saved himself on the very edge of a downward slide. And he breathed a sigh of relief when he reached the top. Now if the day were clear, or he had more of a woodman's training he might be able to strike straight across country for his tower. But with the blizzard hiding most of the landscape, he did not quite dare that. He must retrace a path along the top of the cliff until he connected with that game trail.

Only now he must face the force of the wind, and he had to fight a blast which left him gasping for breath when it met him head on. Blake paused, a little frightened. That had been enough to sweep him off the cliff. He did not dare to keep on in the open.

If the island followed the contours of the one in his own world, the one which was one gigantic city, then it wasn't too long. But half a block in this storm could completely bewilder a man. He should find a tower and hole up, wait for the fury of the wind and snow to abate. Pakahini might think him lost and not search at all and make his scheduled departure. The more Blake considered that idea, the more sensible it seemed. Now—to find a tower...

He could follow the wide way inland which led from the head of the staircase. Sooner or later that should guide him to a tower.

Unlike the scattered, purposeless planting of the towers he had seen, this route ran with a mathematical thrust toward the heart of the island. And he had not gone far before towers did loom out of the murk. But all of these were intact, unbroken, affording no shelter in their round bases. They were also larger than the others. He went on, staggering when the wind struck at him cruelly.

It was cold. Through the slacks, the boots which had been protection enough against storm on his own level, the chill struck him. His hands, covered with the mittens which were attached to the parka sleeves, he stuck into his arm pits, huddling in upon himself, making his wavering way from one rock mass to the next, hunting a hole which was never there.

The shriek of the wind was now deafening. It could have covered the advance of a whole regiment of metal worms and their ogrish owners. Blake paused every few strides to stare about him. But the white blanket rising now well above his ankles showed no breaks.

He came to another flight of steps, broad enough to be a series of ledges. And at the top of that ascent was a wide expanse open to the sky, scoured clean of drifts by the wind. He dared not venture out there, but climbed down once more to make his way about the platform. The pavement ended there; there was no other guide to follow.

Blake leaned against one of the intact towers. The ruins where he had entered this world lay to his left—he had retained that much sense of direction. Should he strike out now that way, trusting to luck to find a den in which to sit out the storm? This couldn't keep up forever!

There was a tower. He could go as far as that one and still win back to this point. Blake made that, then stumbled ahead to the next, to be faced by a wall of thorn bush half-hidden in a snow bank. He could thread his path from one to another, around the barrier of the brush.

He was panting, his head beginning to whirl, when he at last was brought up (literally blown against it with bruising force) against a tower which did afford a refuge. There was a large gap, an opening into blackness. Blake had remants of caution, enough to hold him in the opening sniffing, afraid of another lair. But the foul odor was missing and he stumbled in, scuffing through the charcoal residue which marked the defeat of the fortress. The black dust sullied the snow as Blake perched on a projecting ledge and sat staring dully out into the storm.

But as the chill crept up his body he was conscious of a new danger. Either he must keep moving or have fire. His fine plan for hiding out during the storm was stupid. He should have had more patience, have maneuvered Pakahini into leading him back to the carrier. Now he was lost, without a fire, imprisoned by the storm.

Not yet was he aware of the full extent of his folly. He made himself walk back and forth across the circumscribed space. A certain amount of snow shifted down from time to time from the roofless reaches above, but the walls did hold off the wind.

Time had no meaning, but he suddenly realized that the howling of the wind no longer blasted his ears and when he peered out the snow had ceased. A lull—or the end of the storm? Either way it was a signal, or he accepted it as such, to make the best of the break and start for the carrier.

He was sure he had been heading in the right direction when he blundered in here, or he made himself believe that he had, a little off the direct course because of the brush wall.

The snow was now as high as his knees, and plunging through the drifts was cruelly tiring. Insensibly Blake altered course, choosing a route where the drifts had not formed, protected by towers or trees.

Now and then he halted, not only to rest, but to examine the ruins in search of that particular tower with the fanged top which marked the vicinity he sought. There were strangely shaped pinnacles in abundance now that they were no longer hidden by the storm, but none showed the right outline.

Blake was struggling through a last high drift, making for a cleared space between two towers when his head snapped up and he listened. That frenzied howl was not born of the wind. He had heard it too clearly before—the screech of a hag huntress!

He looked back. Sound was distorted here by echo. Was that cry from one nosing on his own trail? Or had some crone cornered other prey? Pakahini?

The hunter had shown so little fear of the hag and her worm when he had disposed of them to rescue Blake that the latter could hardly believe he would allow himself to be attacked. But suppose a man fell here, it would be easy to break a leg, twist an ankle in this place of ice and snow and rolling stones. And unable to move he would be sure prey for the worm and its mistress.

Pakahini? Blake shifted from one foot to the other. He owed the hunter his life. And if their positions were now reversed and Pakahini needed aid . . . But he could not be sure, perhaps the worm was slinking along behind *him!* And he had no way of deducing from which direction the scream had come.

Sense dictated an advance. But Blake turned back, quartering toward the right, padding into a run wherever the ground was bare enough to allow haste. His breath hissed between his teeth as he listened, over the pound of his own heart, for a second cry.

Here the towers were farther apart, and the tangled bushes between them forced him into wider and wider detours from the track he had marked for himself. Then he started, rubbed his mitten across his eyes, and looked again. He was right! There was the fang topped tower. Chance had brought him back to the very place he was seeking!

And swift upon that recognition came again the howl which had drawn him there. He slowed pace, for with the sound his own warning struck. Danger ahead!

A third howl, so swift on the dying echoes of the other that he was certain it had not come from the same throat. A pack of crones gathering in for an easy kill?

Blake skinned the mitten from his right hand and reached for his dagger; then set the steel blade between his teeth while he looked about him for a rock to hurl. He advanced cautiously, slinking from the shadow of copse to the protection of a pile of rubble, until he rounded the fang tower.

From there a cleared space led with only the thinnest screen of stunted and leafless brush to the tower he sought, the one which hid the carrier. But he forgot about that when he saw what was happening before him.

A fur clad figure was pinned to the ground by the shining length of a worm. And over it struggled, talon against talon, tooth against tooth, two of the hags, tearing and gouging at each other in an elemental determination to each have the kill for herself. In almost automatic reflex Blake's arm went back, and the stone he had found sped through the air to strike against the skull of the nearest with a horrible, hollow sound. The hag he had brained went limp in her opponent's grasp, and the other took advantage of that chance, burying her teeth in the now flaccid throat.

Blake sprang across the clearing. There was a chance that the victim was not yet dead. For the first time in his life he used a knife to kill, experiencing an odd shock as it entered flesh and bit deep into body wall. The hag raised a dripping mouth, gasped at him with wild eyes. He leaped aside as the worm stirred and struck for his legs. Then the wild woman seemed to shrivel in upon herself and collapsed. And the worm remained as it was, rearing to grasp at Blake but not quite making it as the will which had powered it died.

Methodically, as Pakahini had done at their first meeting, Blake smashed the eyes, saw the metallic creature fall clatteringly to the rock. And then he turned to the hunter on the ground. A single glance was enough. Only by the torn and befouled parka could Pakahini be identified now. Even the manner of his entrapment and death would remain a mystery, as Blake could not bring himself to touch that horribly mangled body. Had he come here hunting Blake and been trapped? Perhaps—but now Blake wanted nothing but to be out of this world.

He pulled himself up the tower wall, swung down into the dusky interior. Snow had drifted a little over one corner of the carrier. Mechanically he brushed it off and then dropped down crosslegged before the control with its row of notches. He had no idea where he was or which of those would bring him to a time and place where he could find help, or even manage to survive. He could only guess.

Blake put out his hand to the control. Second notch—a blind choice, but this time if he had made the wrong selection he would *not* allow himself to be separated from the carrier. He tugged the lever loose and pulled.

The lights, sounds, spells of darkness. He closed his eyes against their dizzying whirl. The vibration ceased and Blake sat for a long moment, his hand slipping from the rod. Then he was aware that he, too, was sliding slowly along the platform. He opened his eyes.

He was out of the tower—that was true. But the carrier was canted to one side, because around it rose walls of broken brick from which projected jagged spikes of rusty metal. Overhead was a roof pocked with ragged holes through which a sun shone, a sun without warmth.

Pockets of snow were cupped in the rubble. A trickle of sandy gravel whispered and he whipped around, knife ready. Across a barricade of debris a rat, bloated, obscene, too tame and confident, watched him.

Ruin and desolation. Blake got shakily to his feet and then over a pile of blackened stone. Food. Water. It seemed a long time since he had eaten with Pakahini. He flinched from his memory of the hunter. When he wavered to his feet he was dizzy and he suspected he was close to the end of his strength. Dared he take the carrier on and perhaps plunge into some trap of Pranj's?

The platform had brought him into what was the more cluttered end of an underground room and, as Blake clawed his way through the piles of rubbish which had cascaded from above, he smelled smoke—wood smoke. There was a fire!

It had burned down to a single smoldering brand: the charred wood enclosed by a circle of bricks. Blake stirred the coals to life, feeding the fire from a pile of wood in which he discovered both broken furniture and splintered packing cases mingled indiscriminately. The graceful leg of a period chair puzzled him and he surveyed it dully, turning it about in his hand. He had seen its like in a decorator's shop of his own world. Its presence here hinted at some major disaster. But he was cold, tired, weak, and still suffering from the shock of the last scene in Pakahini's world.

Several blocks of concrete had been placed as if to serve as seats. And in a corner was a pile of ragged blankets and strips of torn cloth which could be a bed. But Blake saw no signs of food, nor could he guess who or what camped here.

". . . sure," the voice shrilled and cracked outside, "he's the one, Manny. We saw him come outta here just before the Limey hider picked him off. Then Ras shot the Limey. He's the one who's been raidin' our cache. . . ."

Blake, in a panic he could not then master, wavered back to the carrier. He made himself small behind a landslide of brick and watched for the arrival of the newcomers. But the fact that they spoke recognizable English was an overwhelming relief.

There was a clatter of feet on stone and a small figure tumbled down through the opening which served as a door. Blake blinked as the other advanced into the sunlight.

CHAPTER TEN

HE WAS a boy, perhaps just into his teens, dressed in ragbag collection of patched clothing. And in the crook of his arm was a rifle ready for use, the muzzle of which swung threatenly as he slowly pivoted to survey the interior.

"Empty," he called. "Jus' as we thought, Manny. He was goin' it alone. We said so." There was a tone of accusation in that.

"Yeah?" The answer from the outside was dubious. "Well, that ain't exactly how the Sarge heard it, kid. And it pays to use your brains, as you oughtta know by now. Ras, you stand guard while we see if we can flush us out another bird."

A second figure entered. This was no boy, but a small, very lean man with gray hair and suspicious eyes alert to every feature of the basement. His arm also cradled a rifle and not one but two knives hung from his belt.

"How long ago did you say that hider picked this guy off?" he demanded, his eyes still cataloguing every detail of the sorry camp.

The boy squinted at the patch of sunlight on the floor as if that were his timekeeper. "Two, maybe three hours ago, Manny. This here fella came out with his water can and the hider sniped him neat. We was on point duty, workin' our way down here for a look-see. Then Ras—he used that ricochet trick you learned us—got the Limey. I did a squirm and saw they was both dead. This fella got it in the head and the Limey took it in the middle. But they both had it—right enough!"

"Then how come this fire's burnin' so good?" Manny asked.

The boy spun around to stare at the flames. "How do I know? We've been makin' point around here for two days now and there wasn't no one here but this one guy—nobody! I did a squirm when he was out yesterday and this place was empty. No sign of another guy holin' up here. I don't care what Long did tell the Sarge— there's only bin one fella here since we've been on point! Go'n ask Ras if you don't believe me!"

Manny scratched a finger through his thick crop of brindled hair.

"Well, you and Ras look around for the cache stuff. I'll take point 'til you're through."

He went out, to be replaced a few minutes later by a second boy not much older than the first. And he too was armed. He stopped short upon viewing the fire.

"How come—?" he was beginning, when the other turned on him.

"Now don't you go on like Manny. He thinks this fella musta had him a buddy."

"But we ain't seen no one else!" protested Ras. His hair

and skin were dark; he was plainly of a different nationality, even race, than his freckled faced companion whose tangled mop of hair was light brown.

"Sure. Only a fire don't lay more wood on itself. Let's look for the stuff and get outta here on the double. I don't like spooky tricks."

They proceeded to the search with a thoroughness and precision which told Blake that this was not the first time they had carried out such a duty. And upon kicking aside the pile of rags in the corner they found what they sought, a loose stone which, when clawed from its place, revealed a cubby filled with tins. Ras gave a sigh of relief.

"That's it. But—looky, he had a lot more'n we thought."

"So that wasn't the first cache he'd tapped!" snapped the other. "We ain't cryin' over gettin' back more, are we?"

He had been pulling the spoil out of the improvised hiding place and now he had a good collection of tins. He straightened up, frowning.

"You go tell Manny," he ordered. "We can't lug all these back to camp—not and watch out for hiders, too."

The gray-haired man returned to inspect the find.

"Good haul. Most of our stuff back again and maybe as much more. No wonder that Limey was gunnin' for him. This woulda been a rich take for a hider," was his comment.

"We can't lug it all back now," protested the younger boy. "We couldn't even pack it across the big hole without help."

"Sure, sure. You take it easy, Bill. Nobody's makin' a pack horse outta you yet, are they? You'n Ras carry what you can. Me—I'll go on point here. If this joker *did* have him a buddy we don't want him comin' back to make trouble by movin' this stuff on us. Get on with it, Bill."

Bill produced a bag which he had carried folded through his belt and stuffed in a collection of tins. Then he went out and Ras came in to copy his action. When Ras had left in his turn, Manny paced restlessly about the cleared space, pausing now and again to listen. He kicked once at the pile of tins, sending one spinning close to Blake's shelter.

"Bait," he speculated aloud. "This here could be bait to bring him back—if there *was* another guy." He took up his position just within the door.

But the cans drew Blake's attention. Food? If he had only had the good fortune to find them first! Manny was alone, but he was armed with a rifle and two knives, and his whole attitude suggested that he knew very well how to use that assortment of weapons.

Blake licked his lips and winced. Food lay only a few inches out of his reach. He longed for the power Kittson had demonstrated days and worlds ago when the agent had drawn the pack of cigarettes across the room to his hand. He could not do that, nor could he enforce his will on Manny as Erskine had manipulated Beneirs. Or could he?

Close to his hand was ammunition of a sort. Blake picked up a brick. Now, if he could get Manny to move just a foot or so! He had managed to use a stone skillfully just an hour back. Blake jerked away from that memory and concentrated on the action at hand.

He fixed both sight and mind on the guard, willing him to walk away from the door—to move a little to the left—just a step or two . . . He must!

Whether Blake's struggles with Pranj had built up his slight psi power, or whether it was only chance, he could not tell, but Manny seemed uneasy. The man kept glancing at the fire now smoldering into coals once more, shifting his feet.

"Bait—" his lips shaped the word plainly enough for Blake to read. "Bait—"

But he did not turn his back on the door. Instead he

sidled to the left, and in that moment Blake hurled the brick. It struck the other on the temple. He gave a startled grunt, falling back against the wall and scraping down it to the floor.

Blake lurched into the open. He could not drag the man away, but he could and did disarm him. Then, scooping up one of those tins, he went to sit on the other side of the fire he again built up.

His prize was an army field ration kit. And he worried off the cover to ram the contents into his mouth. He was chewing vigorously when he noted that Manny's eyes were open and watching him. For some reason the other did not seem surprised.

"You a tech?"

Not knowing whether it was better to claim or deny that label Blake drank from Manny's canteen and waited for another lead.

"You must be—that swell fur jacket and all. We don't get us stuff like that around here. And you ain't no hider; you'd show up too well. You'd be picked off on your first squirm."

Blake glanced down at the parka which was his legacy from Pakahini's world. The fur was a startling black and white and about the skirt of the long tunic was a band of vivid scarlet cloth worked with brilliant threads in the dot and circle patterns of the hunter's people. No, it was not a garment in which one could be inconspicuous. Manny's clothing was drab in shade, fading into the background. Even his salt and pepper hair added to that protective coloring.

"A real live tech! But how'd you get here? Were you livin' with the guy that Limey picked off? Long did say as how he was sure there was more'n one fella holed up here. But if our fellas had seen you before they'd have said so. Say," his eyes lit up as he wriggled into a more comfortable position, "have you guys got planes again?

Them kind what you can sit down right where you want 'em—the 'copters? Baldy reported seein' a big one, but we thought it was likely a Nasty and we took to the deeps for two-three days 'til we was sure they weren't unloadin' any more stuff."

Blake picked that up, it would be as good an explanation for his mode of arrival here as any. "Yes, I came in on a helicopter. But it crashed. Where is this anyway?"

Manny hunched forward. "You ain't a Nasty," he remarked with conviction. "I never did hold with them stories about the Nastys still hangin' around up north somewheres. They never got more'n a toehold, and them last radio messages said that nothin' was gonna come 'cross sea to help them. They sure gave us a pastin' here. You musta seen that when you flew in. But that weren't nothin' to what we gave them back. This here is—" he gave the name of the city.

Blake stopped eating. Of course, inside him, he had known all along that that was true—ever since he had heard the familiar speech of Manny and his crew. Same city—but plainly a different level—though one not so far from his own. This one was in ruins—what had happened here?

"Where you from? I heard once that there was bunches of techs hid out—'way off in the mountains and such places. Sarge has been tryin' to contact them, talkin' about doin' it after we get the hiders cleared out and can live peaceable without gettin' shot at every time we make a move outta our own holes. You a tech scout, eh, comin' down to see what's what?"

Blake decided to agree to that with a nod.

"What happened here?" he dared to ask now, trying to guess how far this level world might be removed from his own. The decision from which it had been born could not be too far in the past. The idiom Manny used was of his own time; the rifle was familiar. This was not an alien as

108

the world into which Pranj had taken him, as the world in which Pakahini hunted his white furred prey and smashed metallic worms.

"Oh, we got plastered in the big raids. Guided rockets and such all over the place. Then all at once they stopped comin'. Guess our boys was givin' them as good as we got," Manny laughed dryly. "Me, I was with the city guard. Would you believe it, I used to push a hack right through these here streets. Seems funny to remember it now—like a crazy mixed up dream or somethin'. Some of the streets ain't even here no more. There's the Big Hole where the subways blew up and then got filled with water.

"Well, I was with the city guard when them Nasty paratroopers came in. We had a bunch of Free British gangin' along with us. And were those Limeys ever tough! Lord, they knew how to scrag the Nastys right and proper! We fought it out buildin' to buildin'. I can't even remember now how it went, so much goin' on a fellow stopped thinkin' and just fought—then hid out to fight again when he'd have a patch of better luck. Time gets so it don't mean nothin' when you're livin' just from one minute to the next.

"First thing I knew I was leggin' it with the Sarge's Mob. He knows his stuff, the Sarge does. You stick with him and you eat, and you live. He's regular army—came out of a hospital when the fight started and rounded up a gang. We was mixed all right: Free British and regular army, city guards, some Navy guys what pulled outta the bombing of the Navy Yard in time, and a bunch of women what could handle a gun as good as a guy. We dug in up around the park and there we've stayed. Them Nastys—we cleaned them up—took us some time to do it proper, though.

"Now we're after the hiders, the guys what went out for themselves and snipe everybody what comes into their territory. Once we get ridda them we can expand like and start huntin' down the things that'll help us start over again. That's what the Sarge's lookin' forward to—startin' up again. Why," Manny's voice was proud, "we growed corn last summer and eatin' stuff in the park. And them deer outta the zoo, we're takin' care of them. Sometime we'll use them like cows—for meat. But mostly we live off supplies we find around." He gestured to the tins. "How's your mob been makin' out?"

"A little better than that," Blake gave what he hoped would be the right answer. He wondered if he dared open another ration tin.

"What th'—!" Manny's bemused stare was aimed over Blake's shoulder, his exclamation made the other's head turn.

The man was staring at the pile of rubble behind which was the carrier. Blake leaped to his feet with a cry of disbelief. Forgetting the other, he plunged forward, climbing over the bricks just in time to witness full disaster.

The carrier was still visible, but around it thickened a wall of green haze; It couldn't be true—there was no one on it at the control—yet it was about to vanish before his eyes!

And the lever moved. No hand held it, yet it was being drawn down in its slot. The green haze curdled fast into a wall. Blake, his heart pounding, watched it shimmer, shimmer and snuff out. The floor of the basement was empty—the carrier had vanished!

"So that there was your crashed plane, eh? Now you just turn around slow and easy, fella. And keep your hands up while you're doin' it!"

The words reached Blake through bewilderment and shock. The carrier was gone; he was marooned! Slowly, dazedly, he obeyed the order. He turned to face Manny, a transformed Manny with the rifle back in his hands, a

Manny who watched him through narrowed and menacing eyes.

"You techs sure ain't very smart, even if you can cook up contraptions like that one what just pulled the disappearin' act on you. Never take your eyes off a fella you've jumped. Now supposin' you take that rat tickler outta your belt and toss it here. And don't try any tricks like you did with the brick or you'll get a bullet right between those big wide eyes of yours what'll finish you off for good!"

Blake tossed the stained dagger blade across the floor. Manny slapped his foot down on the weapon but did not stoop to pick it up. Blake was still more engrossed with the fact that he was marooned; to him it was more important at the moment than the fact Manny was now in control.

"You can sit down," Manny informed him. "Looks like you need to before you fall, but right there on that block and keep your paws out where I can see them. What's the matter with your left one?"

"My shoulder's hurt," Blake informed him dully.

"Huh? Hider get you—or trouble back where you came from? Looks to me like you was makin' a quick getaway from somewhere with that spook flyer."

Blake did not answer. There was no use in trying to explain all the wild events of the past few days. And he had an idea that Manny would not believe any of it, even if he did tell the truth. The ex-hackie had again taken a station by the door where he could not only keep his eye on his prisoner but on the scene without as well.

"Beats me where you come from." Manny was inclined to be talkative. "Wearin' them clothes you ain't no hider. 'Less you found some new warehouse to loot. But you'd be a fool to squirm around with that coat on you, just a sittin' duck for the first sniper who gets sights on you. So you must be a tech. Anyway—Sarge'll get it outta you.

Fellas don't clam up when he says 'talk'; they talk and talk fast. How long you been here?"

Blake stared into the fire feeling nothing but a dull discouragement. Through his adventures, so far, even in Pakahini's nightmare world, he had always been sustained by the feeling that he was, in a manner, in control of the situation, that escape via the carrier was at hand. But now his exile might be permanent. He was certain that Pranj had, in some way, managed to locate the level traveling device and summon it back to him.

"I said, fella, how long have you been here?" Manny's voice carried a snap.

"What? Oh, just a little while; I don't know," Blake replied absently.

"And what was that thing that went off by itself?"

"A new type of transportation."

"Only it wasn't supposed to leave without your being on it," Manny observed shrewdly. "What about it? Set on some sort of an alarm and you didn't get back in time? Now you're stuck here. Well, Sarge'll sure be glad we picked you up. We could use one of them disappearin' machines—we sure could!"

He was interrupted by a shrill whistle, three times repeated. And he puckered his lips to answer it with a single trill. A moment later four of his fellows crowded through the door. Two were the boys who had been there before, the other two were a tall blond man, too thin for his frame, and a Chinese.

"Well, whatta you know!" Bill exploded. "So he did have a buddy!"

Manny shook his head. "This here's some kinda tech. He was tryin' out a travelin' machine. Only it took off and left him stuck right here with the rest of us ruin rats."

All four stared at Blake as if he had suddenly grown horns and a pale blue skin before their eyes.

"A tech!" breathed Ras. "Where'd he come from? There ain't no techs near here."

"You been personally all over this here city?" Manny demanded. "We can go about three square miles—and the rest we don't know. Anyway, you, Sam and Alf, get yourselves a loada cans and help us take this guy back to Sarge. He'll sure be glad to get his hands on a real live Tech!"

The Chinese and the tall man packed cans into bags and then closed in on Blake.

"He's got a bum shoulder and his left fin's no good," Manny informed them. "I took his knife. Hey you, stand up and let Alf see if you have any booby traps under that fur tent of yours."

Blake got wearily to his feet and stood passively for the search. All the other discovered was the sealed jar he had brought from the laboratory. Seeing the demon's head on the knob, Manny promptly ordered that that be presented to the Sarge.

"All right, mate," the blond Alf spoke for the first time, "you move along now—easy does it." He had an accent Blake could not place, but the out of time man suspected that much of the big man's slowness might be a pose.

"Don't get no funny ideas about heavin' no more rocks, neither," Manny warned him. "Sam's a sniper and Alf— I've seen him break a guy's neck for him, usin' just his hands—as easy as snappin' a stick."

One of the boys went out first, rifle ready. Behind him scrambled Manny, then Alf waved for Blake to follow.

The door opening was below the surface of the ground, but a series of toe hollows for steps led them up into the full light of day, a cold winter day. There was some snow, melting where the sun struck full upon it, but even such drifts as he had battled among the towers that morning could not have concealed the awful desolation Blake now faced. Before its fate had come upon it, this city must have been close twin to the one of his own time. Another clue that the decision which had split their time stream levels had been of recent origin.

If he had not been so weary and sick at heart he might have asked questions. But now he dumbly obeyed orders to travel along the narrow path which wound among the mounds of debris.

CHAPTER ELEVEN

THEY SPLIT up as might an army patrol in dangerous territory—the boys scouting ahead. Sometimes they paused while one or two prowled away, taking cover, and they did not march on until a signal was whistled. Blake gathered that the Sarge's "Mob" did not control this particular section of the city, and must move through it ever on guard.

Whole blocks of buildings had been leveled off well above the original position of the street. And in other places there were empty gaps, deep pits in the ground, marked with reed vegetation, some with frozen ponds in their centers. This condition had plainly existed for several years.

Blake deduced that they were traveling uptown, but distances were difficult to measure when it was necessary to make so many detours. Sometimes they took paths beaten through the rubble by steady use, at other intervals they scrambled percariously over barriers of sand and stone.

"Big mess." Sam gave his prisoner a steadying hand as they crossed one such patch.

Blake managed a tired grin. "It sure is."

"No mess, your place?"

"No," was all the reply Blake had breath for.

"Better some day here, too. We got good place. Sarge —he fix."

They came out into an open space between two mountains of torn and wrenched stone. Before them was the lacework of bare tree branches against a very clear blue sky. Blake made a startling discovery—he knew this under very different circumstances. This was the park! And they were about to enter it not far from the road he had taken with the T.V repair truck!

He had been right, he knew this city. But it couldn't be his own level. One did not go forward or backward in time by the route of the successor worlds—only across it. The agents had sworn to that. However, merely because he did recognize it Blake felt a new spark of hope. If he could only discover what historical decision had triggered this!

The party passed a formidable barrier thrown up at what had once been one of the main entrances to the park. Sentries on duty there exchanged news with the party who had been out on a "squirm." But Blake was more intent in trying to pick out landmarks. If he had only known the city better before he had been taken by Scappa's men!

Were the agents tracing Pranj now through the bands of worlds? Had they any information as to which the outlaw fancied, or did they just visit the likely ones? And would they sooner or later appear in this one to investigate?

Saxton had said that certain possibility worlds would attract Pranj, those "disturbed" levels where chaotic conditions fostered dictatorships. Well, this one, judging even by the limited view Blake had had of it, was certainly "disturbed" to a high degree. Enough to attract Pranj and so the agents? He might not be as helplessly lost as he first feared.

Blake was hustled on down a badly kept road toward

the center of the park. He was not in the least surprised to discover that they were bound for the same summer-theater restaurant he had seen in his own time. He glanced at the parking lot. Two battered jeeps rusted in one corner and several large trucks had sunk almost hub deep in the cinders. But there was no TV repair van.

On the other side of the building was a circle of cabin-huts, rude, one story shelters combining in their walls tree trunks and plundered brick and stone—from the chimneys of which puffed blue wood smoke. The taint of that smoke was thick on the air, together with the effluvium of human beings, none too clean, dwelling in a limited amount of space. But the huts were set in a straight line, an equal amount of ground about each, and the settlement had an air of permanence, almost of efficiency, which contrasted sharply with the chaos of the city.

A flag dropped limply from a pole outside the large building: Red, white and blue. Right enough! Yet there was something odd about the way those colors were combined, Blake was not sure that it was the stars and stripes he had always known. Below it was another—a smaller, squared banner which Sam indicated with a thumb as they passed beneath it.

"That belongs to Tenth Cavalry. Sarge—he was Tenth Cavalry in regulars."

They went up the steps and entered what had been the lobby of the theater. Battered desks in a military line occupied much of the space. But only two were now in use. At one sat a man whose scanty hair was white and yet whose shoulders were squared by years of army drill. And at the other was a young man who glanced up from a study of a torn map to survey Blake with astonished eyes.

"Tell the Sarge," Manny swaggered to the fore of his small command, "that we've got us a tech!"

Now the man was attentive, his open wonder plain as he saw Blake's clothing. The girl left her desk and vanished into the auditorium, to return shortly.

"Take him in."

Only Manny and Alf accompanied Blake into the main room. Most of the seats had been ripped out, only four rows close to the stage remaining intact. Crossing that wide expanse of floor, knowing that he was the center of attention, awoke self-consciousness in Blake. On the stage were three more desks, the middle one slightly ahead. Behind it sat the man who must be the ruler of the settlement—Manny's Sarge.

And so impressive was he that he dwarfed the other two men who shared the platform. Blake had met and seen men of assurance since this wild adventure had begun: Kittson and his teammates, the nobles who had visited Pranj in the alien world, Pranj himself, Pakahini. But none of those had been of Blake's world or kind. There existed a difference of which he had always been aware.

The Sarge was no arrogant noble, no psi man a little overpowering with his self-confidence, no hunter of a tribe who dominated his world. Always the superior who dealt only with inferiors when it came to action, the Sarge was a born leader of ordinary men—men like Blake—understandably human, whom chance and the right time had brought into his own.

His assurance held no hint of arrogance; his self-confidence no hint of superiority. He was ready and willing to face any test fate might present. When he looked down at Blake, there was something almost gentle in the smile which revealed strong white teeth, contrasting the coffee brown skin.

"You look," his voice was smooth, warm, "as if you've come a long way, Mistuh."

Blake relaxed. Manny and his men had inspired little

trust. But the Sarge was a different proposition. He might have been Kittson.

"Rather," he replied.

Those dark eyes were assessing his clothing, missing no detail of the parka, of the slacks and boots. Manny stepped up to place the gemmed dagger and the sealed jar before his commander. But the Sarge gave each exhibit only a passing glance.

"You techs robbin' museums now?" he chuckled. "Where you from, Mistuh, up Canada way? Seems like I've seen fur coats like yours from there. On a tour to see how the ruin rats are makin' out?"

"He had some kinda machine. It just disappeared and left him," Manny reported importantly.

The Sarge sat very still, only his eyes moved from the ex-hackie to Blake and back again.

"Plane? 'copter?"

Manny shook his head. "This here was somethin' new. Flat platform, not even a motor I could see. It was in this here cellar where we traced the looter. This tech was hidin' there. Knocked me out before I saw him. Ate rations like he was half starved. Then I saw this green light over in a corner. He looks, too, gives a yell and runs. In the middle of that light was this here machine. Light went off and the machine with it, just snuffed out like a candle."

"At which point you took over, Manny?"

"Sure, Sarge. He was a greenie. Left my gun lyin' right there on the floor for me."

"And now you're gonna tell us how your machine got in that there cellar," the voice was a velvety, cushioned purr. But below its liquid softness was steel. "We could use a neat trick like that ourselves."

Blake saw no possible reply, except an honest, "I don't know how it works."

The Sarge still smiled. "That's too bad, Mistuh. Seems

118

like you techs and the big guys who got theirselves out before the smashup want to write us off as no goods, while you plan the future. Only, we're still around and we've got somethin' to say. Anyway, Mistuh, you're gonna stay here with us for awhile 'til we decide what to do about you. Manny, lock him up."

"He's got a bum shoulder, Sarge. Shouldn't he see Doc first?"

"Huh? You techs fightin' each other now, maybe?" The Sarge laughed as if he found that thought highly amusing. "Take him to Doc, and then lock him up," His eyes moved to the pile of papers before him; it was as if they were now invisible.

"This way, tech."

They did not go back through the lobby, but out a side door into what had once been the restaurant. Here partitions had been set up to cut the large room into a series of cubbys, mostly lighted with candles and oil lamps, though the walls did not reach to the high ceiling.

"Doc around?" Manny demanded of a girl they met just inside the door.

"In his office."

A narrow hall ended in a door which was only a curtain of canvas rigged over a pole. Manny stopped.

"You there, Doc?"

"Come in."

The ex-hackie pulled aside the drapery and waved Blake in.

"What is it now?" The gray haired man at the table did not look up at once from his microscope. "You or one of your boys get punctured by a hider, Manny?"

"No. We just got us a prisoner who needs patchin' up."

"A prisoner!" Now he did turn to view them. "Since when has the Sarge been taking prisoners." Then as his eyes rested on Blake they showed real surprise. "Tech!"

he almost whispered. "By all the Saints, a tech! So they've contacted us at last!"

"Maybe yes, maybe no," Manny poured cold water on his enthusiasm. "We've found just this one and he's on the lam from his own crowd; the signs point to that. Sarge says to patch him up and then put him in storage."

Blake with the doctor's help stripped to the waist, exposing the raw red mark on his shoulder.

"That wasn't made by no bullet!" observed Manny, watching the proceedings with interest.

"Burn," was the doctor's diagnosis. "Almost like some form of radiation."

Blake shivered. In his own time that word had an ominous meaning which allied it with the worst of disasters.

"How did you get it?" the doctor was continuing.

"New kind of weapon," Blake returned. "But it didn't hit me full blast."

The doctor was looking over an array of jars. "Just as well it didn't. I'd say it might have been able to eat a hole through you. Burn . . . sure enough, and we'll treat it like one. We don't," a note of bitterness crept into his voice, "have the wealth of supplies you techs laid up before the smash, but we do our best. See here, Manny, I don't like the look of this. Suppose you leave him with us. I'll bed him down in one of the inner rooms; he can't elope out of there. And I want to keep an eye on him for a time."

When the other hesitated the doctor added impatiently:

"Put a guard at the door if it'll make you and the Sarge any happier. That's the only exit and he isn't going to get past it unseen. And, if I'm any judge, he's in no shape to make a run for it anyway."

Manny shrugged. "Okay, Doc. He's all yours. I'll tell the Sarge that. So long."

Blake watched him go. He was more conscious now of

the constant dull ache in his shoulder. The doctor had started a new worry.

"How bad is it really, doctor?"

"Just bad enough to keep a tech here where I can ask him a few pertinent questions," replied the other. "By the look of you, you've had a pretty rugged time. What would you say to a hot bath, a good meal, and some conversation. Better than being stuck in a detention cell—eh?"

Blake brightened. "Decidedly!"

The bath must be taken in a tin tub supplied by buckets, but it was hot enough to draw the chill out of his bones. And presented with fresh, though worn and patched clothing, he sat down to eat with the doctor, a soothing dressing on his shoulder, really comfortable for the first time in several days.

"Where's your tech headquarters? Somewhere in the north I'd say, from that spectacular fur jacket of yours—"

Blake was greatly tempted to tell the truth. But caution prevailed and he answered with the best evasion he could produce.

"Frankly, I don't know. I was getting away from there in a hurry and landed here. I can't tell you how or why."

The doctor's shrewd eyes met his. "That almost sounds like the truth. You say you were getting away in a hurry. Is Manny right? Are you an outlaw? You have a burn made by an unknown weapon. Are the techs fighting among themselves, or have the Nastys take on a new lease of life and jumped you?"

"Neither as far as I know. I was dealing with—well, you might call him a renegade," Blake began slowly, try-ing to fit facts into a framework the other would believe. "He's trying to set himself up as a dictator."

"Pocket Hitler, eh?" the doctor did not appear sur-prised. "We've had plenty of them ever since the real article stopped riding the air waves out of London. They come and go—just nuisances mostly—"

"From *London!*" Blake seized on the one piece of information which was startling. "Hitler in London! When?"

"Didn't your crowd catch that last broadcast before the 'No Return' attack was launched?" the doctor wanted to know. When Blake shook his head he continued, "Yes, I remember now, things were a bit disorganized along about then and your tech holes were cut off from the rest of us. I was on duty in the fourth district, defense area, then. We heard him screaming out his nonsense. Then he was cut off right in the middle and we knew our boys had plastered London, but right. Never a peep from there since. Someday, maybe five, ten years from now, if Sarge and those like him can get us on our feet again, we'll get a plane into the air or send a ship over and discover what really happened to Adoph and his friends."

Historical decision; Blake concentrated on that. Something to do with World War II; he could pin it down that far. But what decision? Hurriedly he tried to remember fateful points in a conflict now more than ten years behind him. And then thought he might have it.

"Then here Hitler *did* win the Battle of Britain," he half-whispered, forgetting the doctor.

August and September, 1940. This world had taken one fork in the road; his the other.

Later, when he had the privacy to think, Blake lay at ease on a bunk, staring up at a cracked and grimed ceiling far above him. The sounds of the hospital annex were muted, his body warm and well fed, he might have drowsed away the late afternoon had it not been for those thoughts.

Hints and names fell into place now, fitted like a giant jigsaw. "Nastys" were the now vanished Nazis of his own world. "Free British," Hitler's broadcast from London—it was all explained. He knew the history of this ruined city. But he had a suspicion that his strange ignorance might have given him away in part.

"Of course Hitler won the Battle of Britain. Surely even the men of a sector experimental station must know that!" had been the doctor's reply to Blake's impulsive speech. "You are well fed, your clothes are good—except for some incidental wear and tear—better than we've seen for years. You appear suddenly and are ignorant of the plainest historical events. You offer an intriguing puzzle, young man."

Blake squirmed. "I can't explain."

"Your 'can't' is probably nearer to 'won't'," snapped the doctor. "But I'm not going to press you. And I'll accept your story about a renegade tech causing trouble. Mainly because that *does* fit in with a rumor which has been circulating lately. But I'll stake my reputation that you are *not* a tech yourself. Not one of the variety I've known in the past. And right now you are adrift from your own world."

That had probably been intended as a figure of speech. But Blake feared that the doctor had detected the start with which he heard it. How much did that keen-eyed man know, or suspect?

"I wish—" he had begun.

But the doctor was continuing. "Let us assume that you come from a secret project, one which was so well screened that it has been cut off from the outside for some time. I can imagine that one newly emerging from such a cocoon would find a great deal to amaze him. What do you want to ask first?"

Blake accepted that, or fell into the trap, now he was not certain which. The other might not believe that he was a tech, but for some reason of his own, the doctor was ready to provide him with the orientation he needed to function in this world. Blake might have to remain here for the rest of his life and the more he could learn the better.

"What if I don't know any history since—" he had groped for a point which might be common to both of their worlds, "Dunkirk?"

"Dunkirk—the end of May, beginning of June, 1940, the last gasp of Britain," mused the doctor. "Well, early in August the pressure came—air attack all out on the British Isles around the clock. The Nastys wiped out most of the air fields by the end of September. The English used their fleet to try a withdrawal to Canada. We weren't in the war then," he laughed bitterly. "Nothing like being too late with too little. The Limeys managed to bring off some of their fighting men and a few civilians. In October we sent in ships to help. But on the 10th, the Battle of the Channel began and with it the air borne invasion of the islands. And on the 15th, the Japs struck us in the West."

"Pearl Harbor!" Blake supplied but the doctor shook his head impatiently.

"Hawaii had nothing to do with it. The Japs sent in waves of carrier based planes all up and down our west coast. Then there was a howl raised to bring our fleet back from dying England. But San Francisco, Los Angeles, Seattle—they'd had it and good. Japs exploded all over the Pacific. I don't know what happened in Australia; they were still fighting a desperate rear guard action along the salt deserts there last we heard. But invasion forces landed in Alaska and lower California. We beat them back to the sea only in time to get it in the east from German raiders. Mix that with sabotage on a grand scale, and a few other tricks."

Blake, recalling very word of that, moved uneasily on his bunk. That flow of news all bad, and all so close to what might have been true. It was all the nightmare of his own world brought into daylight. And this was no dream—this world was real!

CHAPTER TWELVE

". . . Germ warfare," the doctor had continued. "Though we can't be sure now. There was a virus infection in the second year. About one in five recovered. It could have been planted and it first broke out about the time the Nastys flattened Washington and made two air borne landings: one here and one in the south. We were hanging on by our fingernails right about then and the virus really smacked us into the ropes.

"Then something happened. What, we'll never know unless we can get across to explore someday. We sent a 'No Return' bombing raid—heavy bombers, carrier stuff, everything which could have the faintest chance of making a one way trip to London when we heard that Hitler and his high ranks had gathered there for conquest ceremonies. Maybe we *did* get all their top brass then, broke their chain of command. Or perhaps they went to fighting elsewhere. We always wondered how long their love feast with the Russians was going to last.

"We don't know what happened. Only the Nastys stopped coming over. Their ships vanished from off our coast and their troops here were abandoned. But that didn't happen until everything was in an unholy mess as far as we were concerned.

"That was—let's see—five—six years back. One begins to lose track of time living like this. We'd proved a harder nut to crack than they thought we would be, in spite of virus and everything they could dump on our heads. But you can't keep factories running when they've been largely bombed out of existence, not with a mechanical setup as complex as ours was. Take a city of this size, knock out the gas, light, water, service of supplies, add an epidemic and you have chaos in less than a week—without any assistance of air attack.

"One factory depends upon raw materials brought from a distance and complicated tools transported from the opposite direction by rail. Smash those rails or either source of supply, and you have a factory unable to function. It's easy to upset the applecart in a highly mechanized civilization.

"Communication went. Radios gave out when parts couldn't be produced or replaced, when there were not enough technicians to run them. We have a ham operator here. He spends ten hours a day listening, and for the past two years he's been unable to pick up another signal anywhere!

"Meanwhile in this city, which is the section I can speak of with authority, we had two attacks of the virus. I can show you places uptown black from fire. That's where we burned bodies—not by the hundreds but by the thousands! Those days were nightmares out of hell! And through it all we fought off a paratroop invasion. Since then we've managed to keep alive by being a little quicker on the trigger than the others."

"What others?" Blake had prompted.

"Deserters, Nastys who escaped the mop-up gangs, criminals who took to open outlawry when law enforcement collapsed. They hide out, preying on us, raiding for supplies. We've driven them out of this western section of the city, though they still sneak in to plunder our caches. The Sarge hopes to organize a big expedition which will rid us of them. He made contact with another Mob of Free British just last week. They're over on the government island in the bay and have two useable launches. So they're willing to give us naval support along the shore, if and when. We can thank our lucky stars for the Sarge!"

"Who is he?"

"Old army—really old army of the traditional style. Ever hear of the Tenth Cavalry?"

Blake had not.

"It was a regiment with traditions, could split honors with Custer's famous Seventh. And it was never massacred because its commanding officer was a glory-grabber. They were part of the old Indian Fighting Army with a list of battle honors to make your hair curl. The Indians called them 'Buffalo Soldiers' and they didn't tangle with them any more than they could help. It was one of the first Negro cavalry troops.

"The Sarge's grandfather joined up right after the Civil War, and his father went in as soon as he was old enough. He never thought of any other career for himself, being born into the regiment as were the Roman legionnaires in their day. The Tenth is gone, but the Sarge is still with us—otherwise *we* wouldn't be here!"

Under the rule of the Sarge the settlement in the park had obtained a measure of security. The inhabitants drew on the contents of stores and warehouses for food and clothing. They clung to a shadow of the civilization they could remember and there was already a second generation growing up to whom the park village was the only way of life. And, Blake learned from the doctor, that in spite of lacking that which would have seemed to them several years earlier the necessities of life, they were not only thriving, but cherished detailed plans for future expansion. It was a community on the way back, inspired by the driving will power and genius of one man.

Forseeing the eventual uselessness of rifles for which there was no ammunition, they had made bows. Grain had been planted in the park area, along with seed found in the ruins of a department store. Deer liberated from the zoo and horses from a riding academy were being bred.

Blake, enthused by the doctor's story, could understand the advantages of being a member of this community, of becoming one of the Sarge's "Mob." If he were sure that there was no chance of his ever being able to win back to his own level, he would count himself lucky to stay here.

In the meantime it seemed that he was forgotten by all but the doctor. He slept and ate, and then slept again. But by the middle of the next morning he was restless. Most of the pain had gone out of his shoulder and he was able to use his left hand and arm almost normally. He dressed in the drab clothing provided him and was sitting on the edge of his bunk when Manny appeared in the doorway.

"Hi," his greeting lacked ceremony, "the Sarge wants to see you."

Blake went with him willingly enough. This time the big man was engrossed with a map on which marched a series of small red dots. He was verifying the position of these from some notes on a sheaf of loose and finger marked papers. But he pushed them aside as Blake and his guard came up.

"What's this you been tellin' Doc about a renegade tech?" he demanded.

"He's the one responsible for my being here," Blake returned. "He kidnapped me, I escaped, and landed in this city."

"And this machine? You don't know how it works? Does it belong to this tech, maybe?"

"Yes, it does. No, I can't tell you how it works. I was able to get away on it, but that's all."

"What's this tech's name?" the question came bullet fashion.

"He has several as far as I know—Lefty Conners, Pranj—" The Sarge showed no sign of recognizing either.

"Ever hear of a guy called 'Ares'?"

Memory of a paragraph from an old school book was triggered by that. "He was the Greek god of war—"

"This one ain't no god," the Sarge's smile was grim, "but he sure does mix into war! For about four months now," he leaned back in his chair, locking his fingers behind his head, "we've been gatherin' in a crop of stories about this here 'Ares'. He's been dickerin' with the hiders, tryin' to organize 'em. And we've been told—if the story's straight it's bad stuff—that he's promised 'em some new arms. Now here you come along with a tale of a tech gone to the bad and causin' trouble. Seems like our Ares and your renegade tech might have somethin' in common, don't it now? You say that your man has this new travelin' contraption and a new kinda gun he shot you with. Yeah, it all fits in nice and smooth. Where's this here Pranj or Conners holed up now?"

"I only wish I knew. He's probably not in this city at all."

The Sarge frowned. "But likely he'll be comin' here?"

Blake himself wanted the answer to that. He understood so little about level traveling. If the carrier could only base in one spot, than Pranj might very well turn up in the cellar where he himself had been captured. And Blake had a strong conviction that the platform had, in a manner of speaking, been fixed while the other level worlds had formed and vanished about it during those incredible trips. So, if the carrier materialized on this level, it would do so there. But would Pranj come here? Was he in truth "Ares?" Knowing that Blake had been marooned here, would he come? Or would Blake's presence be an additional lure? There were so many ifs, and Blake felt he could not judge the other's reactions by his own. Pranj was psi—and an outlaw psi at that.

There was one other chance, for himself, for the eventual capture of Pranj. The sight of the map on the Sarge's desk had reminded him of that. What about the agents? Blake had no idea of where their carrier might be located or whether they were now using it to cruise the worlds they suspected Pranj of visiting. But the outlaw's discovery of their warehouse hideout had driven them to Patroon Place. Suppose that move had taken them to their point of contact with other levels. Again. . . If. . . And. . . Maybe. But it gave Blake something to aim at.

"He may turn up in the place where I was found," he said.

"Because you landed there?" the other caught that quickly. "Was that thing you came on set on a homin' device?"

"I tell you I don't know!"

"But you can guess a little, is that it? That the only place you can think of?" The Sarge's voice was lazy, but the deep set brown eyes boring into Blake were alert, almost as compelling as Kittson's had been.

"Well, Pranj is on the run. There're some others after him."

"So?" The Sarge's lids drooped, half-veiling his eyes. "And you would like to meet up with the guys after him? Friends of yours, eh? And where do we go around lookin' for 'em?"

"I'd have to see a map," Blake countered. "And I'm not sure they're here either."

"Cagey, aren't you?" The Sarge pushed back his chair from the desk and beckoned. "Come around and take a look. This here's the best map we got."

The creased paper was torn and had been mended, and there were stains disfiguring its surface. But Blake traced the route he had taken up town by bus. The legend of "Mount Union" had been almost obliterated by a black smear, but he found it and then centered on Patroon Place. Had he been able to tell the full truth perhaps the quest would have been easier. But belief might not have followed his story. They would have to accept him on trust. Or, if and when he could leave this settlement, he must make for that point by himself.

The Sarge looked at the map. "That where these friends of yours hang out?"

"That's where I hope they do," Blake corrected. "But they may not be there. There's only one chance in perhaps a thousand."

"So." The Sarge rested his square jaw on a pile driver fist. "You sure don't tell a man much do you? But we've been bettin' our roles on a hellva lot of slim chances lately. Only maybe we'll take a look at that downtown place first—we know that territory. This," he licked a finger on Patroon Place, "is new; and after all you landed in that other joint."

"When the machine is in use there is a green glow."

"Sure is," Manny broke in for the first time. "Lights up the whole place, Sarge. I saw it."

"In daytime even, eh? Your friends have them a gimmick like that too?"

Blake had to believe that all carriers were alike. "Yes."

"Then we can set two points." The Sarge became brisk. "One down one up. You," he spoke to Blake, "go along with the uptown picket. You know your friends. We can take care of Ares if he turns up. You're going to save us time and trouble all around."

"If Ares is Pranj he's—" Blake began a warning.

"If he's your renegade tech he's trouble with a capital 'T'. Boy," the Sarge laughed, "we don't need no tellin' about that. We've been up against some tough men lately."

But not as tough as the outlaw level traveler, Blake wanted to say. Not against a man who would turn an enemy's brain inside out and control him as if he were a robot! He could only hope that he would reach the agents before the Sarge's men reached Pranj.

So, without being able to impress his warning more

strongly, Blake found himself one of a party organized to explore uptown. He was, however, not offered arms, not even the gemmed dagger Manny had taken from him.

They kept to the overgrown wilderness of the park for their trek west. As they passed the empty cages of the zoo, Blake asked what had happened to the other animals beside the deer. The birds, he was told, had been freed to hang about the settlement, those which had survived the winters. The bears and felines had been shot.

"Not them wolves though," commented one of the men. "We got two hides curin' now. Some run and joined up with the dog packs for huntin'. In winter they're worse'n snipers if a man's alone."

Large portions of the park, which had originally been a long strip of greenery running two-thirds of the city's length, had relapsed into a jungle of matted shrubbery. The once well-kept roads had shrunk to rutted tracks between banks of inpenetrable brush.

They rounded the end of an ice bordered lake, sending waterfowl squawking hysterically into the air, exchanging rude pleasantries with the gang hauling water in tanks. Even about such homely tasks the park dwellers went armed, with either bows or rifles. Blake learned that the rifles were given to those who by marksmanship proved themselves worthy, while less skilled "fighting men" (a category which included all males from the age of twelve and some women) had to be content with bows, though the younger boys had shown so much aptitude with those more antique weapons that they preferred rifles only as a matter of prestige. When the last bullet was fired, the transition to bow would not find the next generation untrained or unarmed.

The purpose of the present expedition was not only to test Blake's theory concerning the agents' base, but also for the regular occupation of foraging. Manny explained how, using old directories of the city and the Sarge's maps, the settlement was able to locate the sites of stores or warehouses which furnished them with supplies. Too often, a promising lead brought them to a district completely burnt out or reduced to hopeless rubble. However, this systematic plan of looting had paid off during the lean years of the immediate past. Every expedition had the glamor of a treasure hunt.

"Drugs for the Doc, material, clothes if they ain't too bad rotted to be any good, tinned stuff—anything what we can use. If we could just move along the streets better, get some trucks runnin', we'd do more," Manny observed. "But when you gotta stop drivin', and break your back every three or four feet luggin' stone outta the way only to run into another pile, well, it ain't worth tryin'. Once we get them hiders cleaned out so as a guy don't hafta keep lookin' over his shoulder every minute or get a bullet in his guts, then we can do this lootin' right. 'Til then we gotta lug stuff in the hard way—mostly on our backs."

"There was a drugstore on the corner of Mount Union," Blake offered.

Three—four days ago he had lingered in that drug store, enjoying its light and warmth, protection against the storm without. But how many years had it been in this world since that building had been able to offer shelter?

"Yeah? Say, maybe we can make this trip pay off good then. Jack," he called over his shoulder to a lanky boy who was arguing with his companion, a smaller Negro lad, "you got that there list of stuff Doc told us to be on the lookout for?"

The boy put a hand into the front of his shabby lumberjacket. "Yessir. Pinned in. Why, Manny?"

"Used to be a drugstore up where we're goin'. If there's anything left of it, you and Bob cut in and see what you can find. Don't try for nothin' but doc's stuff—that's the most important."

"Yessir," the boy agreed and dropped back into the amicable dispute which dealt with the possibility of tracking down the dog pack whose trail had been seen further to the west. Wolf and dog pelts were esteemed goods at the settlement.

"Jack's quick on the uptake. He may learn Doc's business when he gets older," Manny reported. "Sarge is sortin' out all the young ones. Some—they kinda take natural to readin' and writin'—though they all gotta learn that—along with their numbers. Last month he had us haul books over from the library—let us take a coupla horses he thought it was so important to bring back big loads. Sarge says them boys may hafta fight all the resta their lives, but they ain't gonna be more ignorant than they hafta. When a boy shows talent for somethin', well, the Sarge puts him to learnin' that as good as he can now. Someday," Manny's eyes shown with warm eagerness, "when them hiders is all cleared out and we can live without fightin' all the time, then we'll spread out more. Get outta this rat trap and see what's happened to the rest of the country. We was on top once, we'll be again— just you wait'n see!"

Something within Blake responded to that. Given a free hand, a reasonably stable future and these people would build again, build something perhaps better than that which had been blasted from with under them. But how stable would be the future if Pranj broke in here? What if the rumor Sarge had heard was true, and the psi outlaw was importing new weapons—say the heat guns of the laboratory world—to equip mad dog fighters here? Those hiders who resisted the return of civilization would be so armed they could easily wipe out this nucleus of a new world to set up one of their own in which Pranj would be overlord.

At that moment Blake's struggle against Pranj went beyond the personal. It was no longer a contest between the two, a contest in which he felt the inferior, but a war against all that the outlaw psi man stood for. Sarge's people must be left unhampered to work out their own destiny, saved from one who could so easily ruin their hopes. Now he was able to understand the real mission of the agents and the web of protection they tried to spread across the other level worlds, the reason for their grim hunt for Pranj. Each world must be left to stand by itself, to rise or fall by the actions of its own inhabitants, and not be enslaved by an outsider.

If he could not return to his own world, Blake decided now, he must tell Sarge the truth—let him know the full menace facing them. But if it was possible to contact the agents, that must be done speedily before Pranj had a chance to strike here.

They left the park and turned into a street where the rows of houses appeared intact. Even a few windows still held unshattered glass in dusty panes, reflecting the chill winter sun.

"Know where you are?" Manny asked.

Blake halted. He had been here only at night but he was sure they were close to their goal.

"Hey, Manny, there's a drug store for sure!" Jack had scouted ahead.

"Any street signs?" asked Blake.

"Wait—" Jack's voice drifted back. "Yeah, says 'Union'. That's mean anything?"

Blake drew a deep breath. "This is it," he said more to himself than to Manny.

CHAPTER THIRTEEN

To ENTER this Patroon Place was a weird experience. The world of the laboratory, the world of the towers, had both been so far removed from the things which he knew that Blake could accept them. But here, where he had been before (or so it seemed), it was different. The same house, the same street—yet here was desolation, the desolation of the long abandoned, the ruined. Broken window panes, battered doors, were everywhere.

Manny jerked his thumb at one. "This here was raided," he remarked. "Rich joints like that got it bad from the looters in the early days. Which house you want?"

Blake stepped into the drive and gazed up at the right house, the exact counterpart of the one in which he had left the agents on his own level. To all appearances, save for the evidences of violence and time, it was the same. He felt as if he walked slowly through some nightmare. The nagging idea that this *was* the same house, that somehow he had traveled forward or backward in time instead of across it, persisted. He shivered as he advanced.

The front door was gone and there were scars about it.

"Bullet holes," Manny identified matter-of-factly. "Guy in here musta put up a scrap."

Within, a barricade of broken furniture fronted them. From somewhere Manny produced a battered flashlight, and its circle of radiance picked out a pile of white bones in the far corner. For one sickening moment, Blake wondered if that could be—? But this wasn't the same world, he must keep reminding himself of that.

"What are we huntin' for?" Manny wanted to know.

"Should be in the cellar," Blake gave a half answer. Since the site of the carrier must be hidden, it would be most easily concealed there—as Pranj's had been.

Manny went from room to room, opening the few doors left. There were other bones, many signs of a battle fought from room to room years before. Once the ex-hackie turned the light on the floor and Blake saw the track of an animal boldly printed in the dust.

"Wolf . . . or dog. They roam about uptown."

"What do they live on?"

"Us—when they can get at us," Manny replied flatly. "They do run deer and horses. That's why we don't go out alone in winter, and why we take cover at nightfall 'less it's an emergency. We've found the remains of hiders that weren't lucky or smart. Cal took the body of a dead pony up to the far west end of the park for bait four, five weeks back. He got him five dogs and a wolf before sun down. They're mean and vicious and smart, too, and gettin' even smarter. Here's the cellar—"

The last door he had opened gave on a flight of stairs and they descended into heavy gloom. A wine storage section, its contents smashed and plundered by the early raiders, lay behind another shelved space where dusty, empty jars stood in rows. They passed through a laundry and a furnace room to come to the last door of all. Manny had been counting paces under his breath, and now he said:

"This here cellar's bigger than the house. I'd say this part's out under the front yard, maybe runnin' out under the street."

Blake's spirits rose. The need for extra space was promising. Space for what? A base for a carrier?

Manny pulled at the door, but it failed to give as the others had done.

"Locked!"

Blake joined in the effort to force it. But it *was* locked, and the heavy wood did not yield. Blake ran one finger across a hinge and brought it away slick with oil. There could be only one reason for oiling a door in a long deserted house. His guess had been right, this was a transfer point for the agents. He had only to keep watch here and sooner or later he could contact them, be able to return to his own world. But that would mean camping here, a cat at a mousehole. And would Sarge and his men permit that?

"Oiled? Your friends, tech?"

"I hope so. But I don't know when they'll be back."

"We'll set up a point here," Manny declared. "If they show, we'll know it. Why in cellars?" He added that last question as if he were thinking aloud, and Blake did not try to reply.

That shrill whistle which was the rallying call of the Sarge's forces sounded as they climbed the cellar stairs. Out in the yard were the remainder of the party, Jack and his younger companion with filled bags on their backs, the taciturn Gorham peering into the garage.

"Say, Manny," Jack greeted them, "that store's hardly been touched! We've got loads for the Doc and there's canned food, too. Worth sending a horse for. Tell Sarge that."

Manny glanced at the sky. It was well past noon by the position of the pale sun. "We grub now," he decided, "then Bob and Gorham pack back to camp and see if the Sarge thinks it's worth sendin' up a horse. We gotta set a point here—you can tell Sarge that. Afterwards, Jack, you sort out the food down at the store. Some might be left to grub the point—save 'em luggin' in supplies. There's some scoutin' to be done. How about it, Gorham, any sign of hiders?"

Gorham shook his shaggy head. "These places were raided, sure, but back in the early days. Lots of things smashed but not much taken. I'd say nobody's been back since."

"We're in luck, then." Manny sat down on the back steps. "Let's eat."

They chewed the rations they had brought with them and drank from the canteens of purified lake water they all carried. A flake or two of snow sailed lazily through the crisp air. Gorham inspected the gathering clouds. "Gonna get it by night," he warned. "Look at all that dark in the east!"

There were billows of dark gray gathering there, piling up in an ominous barrier. Blake thought they might promise a real storm. If the party was trapped in such a one they might be prevented from establishing a post here. Perhaps Manny had the same thought, for he moved uneasily and finished his meal with a couple of hasty gulps.

"Gorham, you and Bob better hit the trail," he advised. "If you can get a horse, cut back here on the double and strip that store. We don't want to get caught out in a bad storm. Jack, go down to the store and pile up stuff for easy packin'. Me, I'm gonna take a little squirm. H'm," for the first time he remembered Blake, "you go 'long with Jack."

That had the ring of an order. Blake wanted to stay right where he was; at any moment the agents might appear. But he was unarmed and his status, free and easy as Manny and the rest had been all morning, was still that of a prisoner. He lingered as long as he could, watching Gorham and Bob depart and Manny slip away into the backyard of the next house. Jack hovered impatiently and *he* had a rifle.

"Let's get going!"

Blake whirled. The sensation of immediate danger struck him like a bullet. For a moment he stared at the silent house, at the yard. Something was wrong—horribly wrong! Danger was building up to an explosive point, behind him!

With a wordless cry he flung himself at Jack, grabbing the boy by the shoulder, jerking him away from the house. Jack twisted in his hold to fight. But Blake, losing his balance, went on in a lunge which caried them both into the garage, and so saved both their lives.

There was a roar of ear-splitting sound, a flash of fire, and the world seemed to fly apart about them. Blake heard a scream of half-fear, half-pain, and then, deafened, half-conscious, he lay where he was and waited for the end.

Dust filled his eyes and mouth, choking and blinding him. He sat up and wiped his hands across his face, blinking tears which cleared his smarting eyes. There was a dull humming in his head, but through it he became aware of moaning.

Jack lay face down, his lower legs pinned under a timber, a splotch of red spreading across one thigh. Slowly Blake turned his head. Where the house had stood, there was now nothing but a ragged hole in the ground.

He crawled over to the boy and went quickly to work. The timber could be levered off, but beneath it was a raw, torn wound where metal had cut deep into the flesh. Blake labored to stop the pumping blood. He was almost sure the bone was intact and that the damage was confined to that tear.

"What—what happened—?" Jack's voice was thin, his hands swept through the dust and debris. "My rifle, where's my rifle?"

The weapon was nowhere in sight. And Blake was in no mood to search for it at that moment. But his viewpoint changed a minute later when the crack of a shot broke the silence which had followed the explosion.

"Two—three—" he counted aloud as the sharp clap of rifle fire sounded through the curtain of falling snow.

Either Manny or Gorham and his companion had run into trouble.

"Rifle—" Jack pulled himself up on his elbows, "Hiders—"

Blake investigated the wreckage feverishly, now as eager as the other to find the gun, but he also ordered:

"Lie down! Get that blood started again and we're licked!"

Jack's knowledge of Doc's trade was a help, for now he obeyed at once, turning his head only to watch Blake's hunt. The rifle showed at last, unharmed as far as Blake could determine. With it in his hands he felt more secure, prepared to face whatever might come at them out of the swiftly gathering murk of the snow storm. With the explosion, his sense of warning had vanished and he thought that for the present they were safe.

"What happened?" Jack asked again in a firmer voice.

"I'd say a bomb went off."

Jack accepted that calmly. "If it was one of those delayed action babies, we were lucky." Again he raised his head for a survey. "Say—the house is gone!"

"Yes." But Blake was more occupied with the present than the immediate past. He could not leave Jack now, and the snow was growing thicker. Although the garage had saved their lives from the blast, it was no proper shelter in a storm. These shots might mean that the rest of their party were dead; that hunters would be out to sniff along their trail. He looked down the street.

The adjacent houses had suffered from the blast. And if they were cut off from the settlement in the park, they would need more than shelter; they would need food, warmth, and medical supplies. There was just one place to find those. Blake was on his own again, in a strange world, an in addition responsible for Jack.

"Look here," he turned around. Jack lived in this world, he knew all the risks, could face a dark future squarely. If he had been tough enough to survive until now, he was tough enough to assess the present odds. "Do you think that with my help you can reach the drug store?"

He saw the boys' tongue move across his lips and Jack did not answer at once. When he did it was to ask a counter-question:

"You think Manny's had it?"

"How can we know? But the storm's growing worse and we can't spend the night here."

The snowfall had powdered the broken sidewalk, was beginning to build drifts around corners.

"Okay. And the store's tight," Jack agreed. "Sure, I can make it. A guy can do anything he has to." He repeated the last as if it were an axiom which had become a law of his kind.

But had Blake known what that trip would entail, he might never have tried it. Theirs was a snail's progress, interrupted by frequent halts to inspect the improvised bandages on Jack's thigh, to make sure that the bleeding had not broken out afresh. Taking most of the boy's weight, Blake was weaving with fatigue as they reached the store. But he got Jack inside to a storeroom in the back before he sat with hanging head, each breath drawing a knife of red hot agony through his side.

Outside, the snowfall had assumed blizzard proportions, curtaining the broken show windows, piling on the floor at the front of the long room. But where the fugitives sheltered, both roof and walls and even two small back windows were in good condition.

"Even if they weren't shot," Jack said suddenly, "the gang's going to have a tough time getting back through this."

Blake realized that his companion still hoped for rescue. But he had something else to ask.

"Won't this storm drive hiders to shelter, too?"

"Should," Jack returned. "Too easy to blunder into a shell pit or one of those places where the old gas and water mains blew up. We generally keep under cover in storms."

Blake regained his breath. And now he began to forage, blessing the custom which dictated that the wares sold by a "drugstore" be so varied. One box gave up a pack of pink and blue baby blankets, and with these he made up a pallet on the floor and, having re-dressed Jack's leg with supplies at hand, settled his patient in some degree of comfort.

When he spoke of the necessity of a fire, Jack objected. The light would attract the very attention they must avoid. But Blake pointed out that the length of the store which separated their hiding place from the street and the heavy fall of snow would hide the flames; and they must have warmth.

The marble top of the soda bar had been broken in pieces by the first raiders of years ago. He was able to pry out one section and drag it into the back room for a hearth. Wood torn from cases provided fuel and he piled it up by the armload.

Meanwhile Jack sat up and sorted through supplies he had gathered earlier, setting apart those they had immediate use for. Blake, on impulse, brought a cigarette lighter from the wreckage of the display case toward the front, and tried to ignite the crumpled pasteboard he was using as tinder. To his surprise the tiny flicker of flames answered and caught. When he was sure the fire was going well, he went back to scoop up containers of snow, using tall soda glasses, pans, anything which would hold this promise of water.

Into a pan from the lunch counter, now full of snow water, he dumped cocoa, sniffing the resulting odor with a feeling of well-being. Jack lay back under the incongruous covering of blankets patterned with cavorting panda bears, and there was a ghost of a smile on his drawn face.

"We're sure covered with luck to have it so good," he observed. "Why, we couldn't have it better at camp." He moved and a twitch of pain crossed his face.

"Leg hurting again?"

"Just when I forget and kick around. And I'm not going to do that. Brother, if Manny and Bob were only here, this would be first rate—just super! What's in that one?"

Blake read the label on the can he had picked up. "Bean soup. That's good. Wait 'til it's heated."

He emptied the contents into another pan, added a small portion of water and set it to heat. Then he poured half the cocoa into a mug and gave it to Jack. The warmth of the fire and the hot drink revived them. But their ease was swept away an instant later.

A howl, low and mournful, carrying even through the deadening curtain of the snow storm, pierced the gathering night. The liquid in Jack's mug slopped over his fingers when that cry was answered by another. His hand went out to the rifle he kept beside the pallet.

"The pack!"

Blake had only the other's concern to warn him, though that howl had sent a trickle of cold down his spine, man's age-old reaction to the cry of a hunt in which he too often had been the quarry. He must know what they could expect.

"Will they attack us?"

"The fire—they don't like fire," Jack admitted. "And they can't get at us except across it. But—" his teeth closed upon his lower lip before he added, "I have only ten shots left."

Blake got up. If the fire must be their main defense, it was up to him to keep it burning. He went out and began harvesting all the flammable material he could find in the

144

store, stacking some of it so that Jack could feed the flames from where he lay. During his quest Blake discovered another storeroom which held mainly cartons of food, and he ripped open the cases hastily, throwing their contents on the floor, adding the boxes to his haul. There was a door there, but it was locked with a bar across it. He did not stop to explore, but he was sure that it opened upon a delivery alley in the back. One of his best finds was a hammer, which had been used to open cases, the clawed end unusually long and heavy. Blake slung it in his belt. In close fighting it would be a nasty weapon.

He was crossing the main room with as much wood as he could stagger under when he glimpsed movement by the street door. Running the last step or two, he hurled his burden into their quarters and then turned to investigate. A dark shadow slunk through the snow. It had been a dog . . . or—?

Outside, the wind whistled, driving snow before it. Blake watched the door, striving to see what might lurk in the street. He could smell the steaming soup; was its scent drawing those shadows? But the fugitives had to eat and Jack needed the warm food—he could not move about to avoid the clutch of the cold.

Somewhere, not too far away, there was a rumbling crash. Blake stepped back into the firelight.

"The wind" Jack's voice kept up the brave pretense of life as usual, "it's bringing down pieces of the ruins. That always happens in a storm."

Blake's eyes went to the roof over their heads, but it showed no cracks. And he knew that the store was well away from any taller building. At least they were safe from being buried alive, no matter what other danger the night and the storm could loose.

He was restless, unable to settle down except for short intervals. Having stacked the firewood, he busied himself bringing in cans and jars of food, until they were well prepared to stand siege. Jack drifted off into uneasy slumber and Blake took up the rifle. He was sure that the shadows flitting around the outer door were real, that only the fire was holding them at bay. So he fought his drowsiness and kept up the flames, plagued within the past hour by a faint trace of the old uneasiness. It did not stab him with the sharp thrust of immediate danger, but he was certain that there was trouble brewing, a more serious trouble than that offered by the slinking pack in the street.

The wall, which formed the back of the store, was broken only by two small windows close to the ceiling; Blake pulled boxes under the nearest, building a vantage point. He climbed, to crouch with his nose pressed against the icy glass, his hands cupped around his eyes to shut out the light. But beyond the pane was only dark and the snow which whispered as it fell. He tried to remember whether the store was situated so that he could see Patroon Place from this back window, and he rather thought that it was.

Now the wind was dying and with it some of the fury of the snowfall. Jack awoke with a cry, as if he didn't know where he was, and Blake went back to him.

"Wolves!" the boy's eyes, too bright, too wide in the firelight, did not quite focus on Blake's face.

"Not here," the other returned soothingly.

Jack's face was flushed and Blake's testing fingers found it hot. He went to the packets of medical supplies. Antibiotics . . . But did this level have the miracle drugs? There were no familiar labels on the bottles he held up in the firelight.

He was still examining the array when he was startled.

Was it a vibration in the air, to be sensed only by one who had known its like before? That strange flash of weakness, the feeling of disorientation, of whirling away—! Blake got to his feet and lunged toward the box stair. He scrambled up and tried to see through the dark. Had he in that moment caught the distant hum of a carrier voyaging between worlds?

CHAPTER FOURTEEN

HAD BLAKE been alone he would have dashed into the night, back to Patroon Place. He did come down from the pile of boxes with a rush which toppled several from their places, but when his eyes encountered Jack he stopped.

He owed no allegiance to Jack—to this world. But he could not walk out of here, even if he were positive that such a move would return him to his own place and time.

Jack's eyes were open and this time the boy was semiconscious.

"The pack—they're going. Manny—Manny's coming!"

Was that true or only a dream which had held into Jack's waking? Before Blake could stop him, the boy's lips shaped that whistle which was the signal for Sarge's men. There was a faint noise from the other room.

One of the pack? Or some man? Blake snatched up the rifle, squeezing past Jack's pallet to search the gloom beyond. Could the agents be exploring? Holding to that faint hope, Blake went into the main room of the store.

A black shape close to the street entrance padded away, another slinked in its tracks. On impulse Blake picked up a can and hurled it after that retreat. There was a startled bark, and a third invader leaped into the night, sending snow fountaining from a drift across the doorway. The pack were withdrawing. Why? Because of his movements, or because they did not wish to face some new menace?

Blake was uneasy, but his private warning was not working. Though he lingered in the outer room for a while, none of the pack returned, and at last the cold drove him back to the fire. No one had answered Jack's whistle. But that did not prove that some hider had not marked them down, and was that very moment creeping up on them with the craft taught by years of such employment.

The night wore on leadenly. Blake kept the fire going and did sentry duty, rising to pace the end of the outer room whenever sleep dogged him. Toward morning Jack's uneasy and feverish sleep deepened into real rest and the boy's skin was no longer so hot. Blake knew a weary relief when dawn grayed the sky and brought a pale light into the cluttered room.

Snow melted in pans and he prepared a hot meal, soup, stew—the most filling food he could find among the cans. The two of them could hold out, he reckoned by supplies, for a week or more. And in that length of time the Sarge should send a rescue party whether or not Bob and Gorham got back to the settlement.

"Smells good!" Jack surveyed the warming food wistfully.

Blake washed the boy's hands and face. His nursing had few refinements but Jack submitted to his ministrations with a sigh of relief.

"The pack still out there?"

Blake shook his head. "They moved out in the night. I don't know why."

Jack frowned. "That's not natural."

But Blake refused to worry about the pack now. "If you can stay alone for awhile, I'll go out the back door and look around."

Jack glanced at the rifle Blake had left leaning against the pile of boxes. Blake smiled. "I'll leave that with you. I have this," he displayed the hammer.

"Maybe you can find Manny. You don't have to worry about me, I have the fire and the rifle. I'll do fine—"

Blake couldn't suppress a yawn as he held a mug of soup in both hands.

"Shouldn't you get some sleep?" asked the other. "I bet you didn't sleep any last night."

"No."

Jack was right; he needed rest. And an hour or two of sleep now might mean all the difference later on. If they were to hold the fort here for another night, he must be prepared to stand guard during the dark.

Exploration of storage boxes provided him with padded beach mats, the makings of a second pallet. And he curled up on it, having given Jack strict orders to call him at the first hint of trouble.

But sleep came only in fitful snatches. It was as if his precognition had been triggered below the level of consciousness. At last he gave up the struggle, heated food for them both, and decided to take advantage of the daylight and explore. Also, before nightfall, he must gather more firewood.

A last trip through the store rounded up all flammable material he could wrench loose. And the number of tracks in the snow inside the entrance were a mute warning not to be disregarded. Blake was not woodsman enough to judge the number of animals making up the pack or to distinguish one set of prints from another. But the beaten space they had left was sobering, and another day of hunger might drive the beasts to the point where fear of fire would not balk their attack.

Blake forced the lock on the back door, leaving Jack, the rifle across his lap, braced against a box, close enough to the fire to feed the flames, with food and water within easy reach. The boy urged him to go. He was certain that Manny was in some trouble and that Blake could find and help him. Blake agreed to this as a soothing measure but he was convinced that if the explosion had not brought Manny back the day before, it was because those shots had made sure that the ex-hackie would never return.

He did not go far from the store at first, conscientiously hunting wood and dragging it back to the stack within, calling out cheerfully to Jack and being answered with the same determined lightheartedness. But all the time he was curbing his impatience to be away—to get to Patroon Place and see if there was any indication that the agents had been there the night before.

"I'm going to go back to the house," he told Jack at last.

"To hunt Manny? That's great! I'll be all right. I have the rifle and the fire and you won't be away long."

"No. I'll make it a quick trip."

As he left the store, Blake's attention roved over the street and the houses. He kept to cover. There were tracks in the snow left by the pack, making aimless patterns. But there were no signs that any human being had walked that way since the end of the storm. The sky was clear and the day crisply cold. His hands, covered only by the crude mittens of the settlement, were numb and he beat them against his sides as he walked, wanting the parka's warmth.

There was the house, or rather the blast hole where yesterday it had stood. Blake broke into a trot, floundering through drifts across the drive.

Then, seeing what was written on the snow, he stopped short. These were no paw marks, but the tracks of men, and they came out of the cellar hole: out of the hole—to go back into it. He stared at the evidence dully, trying not to believe that it meant he was too late.

The footprints were anonymous. He could not be certain that any of them had been made by Saxton, or Kittson, Hoyt or Erskine. But they took him straight to the edge of the cellar and he stared down into the jumbled wreckage. Here the snow was scuffed, pushed away by the passage of feet and bodies. But on one flat surface was the final answer. More prints—tiny, distinct, made by a kitten, and ending abruptly where someone had gathered up their maker.

Black depression settled upon Blake. They had been here last night! He had been so close, so very close and now—. He kicked at a brick, sent it flying into the hole. They had not lingered; they were gone, which might be because they saw no reason to explore here—that they would not come back. He had missed his one chance!

His frustration flamed into anger. But that did not last when he heard the crackle of rifle fire. He spun around, knowing that he was not the target. Loud as they were, those shots had come from some distance away—the store!

Blake ran down the street, skidding in the snow, the hammer ready in his hand. Jack was alone. Another shot informed him that the end had not come. He rounded into the alley onto which the back door opened. No one here. The door was as he had left it. They must be attacking from the front. He clawed open the door, skirted the woodpile and made for the main room.

"Jus' one—a kid—an' he's hurt." The voice rang hollowly through the wrecked store.

"Sneak up on him."

On the floor, just within the streetdoor, a man lay on his face and from beneath his body trickled a dark stream. But two more were on their feet, plastered against the walls, out of line of Jack's fire. One held an automatic, the other a knife.

Blake's eyes narrowed. The knife man, luckily was on the other side of the room. But the gunman had crept by where he was crouched. A slim chance—but perhaps their only one. Gathering his feet under him like a cat,

Blake sprang, the hammer up for the single blow luck might give him.

Something made his quarry half turn and the blow did not land true, but struck glancingly, the claw of the hammer tearing loose a flap of flesh above the man's ear.

With a scream, he staggered back, one hand to his head. But he did not drop the automatic and a shot burned by Blake's jaw. There was a hoarse shout from the other side of the room as Blake threw caution to the wind and jumped to strike a second time.

The man went down, in silent limpness, flopping to the floor as might a doll from which the sawdust had been drained. Blake whirled, but not to face attack. The knife man had remembered in time that in going to his fellow's defense he must cross Jack's line of fire, and he showed a healthy respect for the boy's marksmanship.

For the moment it was a stalemate. Then Blake noted the automatic his victim had dropped. With that in his hand he would be in command of the field. But the man across the room knew that too. His bearded lips snarled; his eyes darted from side to side. When Blake moved, so did he, scrambling to safety behind a counter.

"Look out!" Jack called. "There's more of 'em!"

Blake went to earth behind a barrier of his own and glanced uneasily at the street entrance.

"How many?" he asked, estimating the chance of crawling from one point of protection to another and so joining Jack. Or would it be better to stay where he was to meet opposition when it came?

"... don't know," was Jack's discouraging reply.

If there were more of them why hadn't they arrived by now? Had the rest of the gang gone on, or were they otherwise engaged? If they had gone beyond earshot the knifeman must be prevented from escaping with his story.

Blake's line of crawl took a new direction as the knifeman sprinted from one counter to the next. Blake snapped a shot which tore a splinter from the floor—too late.

The counter line ended a good distance short of the door. If the man was planning to run for it, he would have several feet of open to cross. This would be a test of patience. Unless the others Jack warned against came to investigate, Blake was inclined to wait.

There was the crash of broken glass from the counter concealing the knifeman. Was he heading to the door? Blake steadied the automatic across his arm. But the hunted did not make the expected dash for freedom. Through small sounds, the crunch of broken glass, a rustling, Blake knew that the man was moving. And since it was not to the entrance, he must be heading back, probably trying to find a position from which he could launch an attack at Blake.

For a while Blake hesitated. Should he move to meet the other, or remain where he was to cut off his escape? Either choice might prove the wrong one. But the frustration which had built up in him since he had learned of the agents' visit spurred him into action. He began to edge toward the rear of the long room.

"Look out!" Jack's shout of warning froze him.

Blake had just time to get to his feet and plant his shoulders against the wall before the knife wielder was on him. The blade skinned across his shoulder and the fist holding the weapon struck hard upon the half-healed burn. The agony of that shook Blake long enough for the other's fingers to vise about his wrist so that he could not use the automatic.

They went down to roll from behind the counter out onto the littered floor until they brought up sharply against the skeleton of a table. Blake kicked out, the point of his boot bringing a grunt of pain from the other. But his gun hand remained locked in an iron grip. The knife! The man's other hand was empty; he had dropped the knife!

With renewed spirit, Blake worked to twist his wrist free as the other brought up his knee in a vicious in-fighting jab, grinding it into the pit of Blake's stomach, expelling his breath in an explosive gap. Paralyzed with pain he sprawled, staring up as the other raised the automatic for a finishing shot, his mouth split in a sadistic leer. He was prolonging the moment of the kill for the pleasure it gave him, as one portion of Blake's numbed mind realized.

But the man's preoccupation with his helpless prey undid him. For the rifle cracked first. An almost ludicrous expression of surprise crossed his face. He coughed and blood spurted over Blake. But he was still conscious, conscious and hating. He put the barrel of the automatic against Blake's forehead, his finger was on the trigger. Blake summoned up his last rags of strength and heaved. He was deafened by a shot and the room darkened and spun around him.

"Please . . . please. . . ."

Words coming out of the mist, hurting his head. Blake's eyes opened. He saw far above him cracked plaster. Frowning, he tried to remember. Where was he? How had he come—?

"Please. . ." the monotonous plaint compelled him to move.

He ached, his whole middle was a red pit of pain, but he pulled himself up. Another body lay across his knees, pinning him to the floor, and his chest was sticky with blood. He'd been shot!

Still gasping for breath, he tugged and wriggled free of the body and then he heard a dragging sound. Pulling himself by his hands, pushing the rifle before him, Jack was making a painful progress out of the storeroom. With the inflection of a prayer, he repeated over and over his "please," his terror filled eyes on Blake. But when the latter sat up, Jack huddled together, giving vent to long shuddering sobs.

Although it was still torture to draw a deep breath, Blake took stock of his injuries. The blood on him was not his own. But he could hardly move his bad shoulder and the numbness spreading from the burn there was effecting his arm. It was an effort to act—but time was important! Jack had said there were more of these jackals. But at least these three were safely dead.

"They—they have Manny." Jack got out the words between sobs and his eyes were naked with appeal.

"How do you know?" Blake crawled over to the boy, wincing as his palm came down on a splinter of glass. He was afraid to try walking; the walls still showed a tendency to whirl when he straightened.

"Went by—outside—prisoner." Jack was regaining control. "Saw fire—three of them stayed. I shot the first one in the doorway; then they split so I couldn't see them . . ."

"You're sure it was Manny they had?" Blake persisted. He put his good arm about Jack's shoulders and supported the boy's shivering body.

"Who else could it be?"

But Blake still wondered. "You didn't see his face?"

"No. I was surprised, the snow muffled their steps. They were past almost before I sighted them."

"And you're not sure how many there were in the gang?"

"I don't know whether three of four went by before these turned in. They'll be back!" His fingers tightened convulsively on Blake's sleeve.

"If they do, they'll regret it. We're ready and waiting this time." Blake's hand went gingerly to his aching middle and then he wished he had not made that experiment. "Look here, Jack, you've ripped your leg open again—"

There was red seeping through the bandage.

"Now we'll see to that first."

Somehow he managed to half-carry, half-drag the boy back to the pallet and tend the reopened wound. Ordering Jack to stay put, Blake searched the bodies in the outer room. It was a nasty job, one he might have shrunk from a week earlier. But this world certainly hardened one fast.

The body by the door was equiped with both a knife and a shotgun. Blake speculated as to why the man had not made sure of Jack with blast from the very start. The automatic now thrust into his own belt appeared to be the sole weapon of the man he had downed with the hammer. But when Blake found the knife the last man had used, he shaped a whistle: the hilt was gemmed; the jewels were a sparkling fire. And he had once had the twin of this. It had come from the laboratory world. Limping, Blake turned and gave a closer examination to each dead face. But their tangled beards were real. There was no indication that they were anything but this world's equivalent of Scappa and his goons. Pranj had his forces on each level, and they must be pretty much of a type. Perhaps the finely dressed, arrogant noblemen of the laboratory level were the Scappas of their world.

He went back to Jack. "Ever seen any of these men before?"

The boy was surprised. "They're just hiders. Look alike, all of them."

Blake showed him the dagger. "One of them had this. Seen one like it before?"

Jack ran a forefinger over the hilt. "Out of a museum?" he asked doubtfully. "Sarge had one something like this, one of the scouts brought it in from a museum. But it was too old, the blade snapped when he tried to use it."

"I think it is proof that these men have been in contact with the renegade tech."

"But the hiders working for him are downtown."

"One reason to bring them up here," Blake spoke his thoughts aloud. "They're hunting for the agents' base—they must be!"

"It doesn't matter why they came," Jack said impatiently, intent on his own problem, "they have Manny. He wasn't even hurt bad, because he was walking. We've got to get him away from them. You don't know how they treat us when they take us alive. And Manny—he's the kind who'll stand up and dare them to do it!" Jack's face was gray. "I can't get away on this bum leg. But you can go—you've got to go after them and free Manny!"

Blake looked down at the shotgun. How was he going to explain to Jack the possibility of doing what he asked? Three, maybe four armed men who knew the city and its ways better than he did: they could take cover anywhere and pick him off long before he caught up with their trail. And with his left arm close to useless again, he dared not just start off into the blue. To say nothing of the folly of leaving Jack helpless and alone.

"You going after Manny now?"

Blake raised his head. "I don't see how—" he began and then was interrupted by a sound which left him wondering if he wasn't dreaming all this.

The faint cry from the outer room came again, fretful, demanding. Blake got up and went to the door. It was true—his eyes supported the evidence of his ears.

Picking her way daintily through the debris, heading straight for him, came a well-fed black kitten!

CHAPTER FIFTEEN

BLAKE HELD out his hand and the kitten approached to sniff at his fingers. But it was only when he touched that soft woolly fur that Blake believed his eyes. He turned to Jack eagerly.

"Are you sure the man they had was Manny? What color was his hair?"

Jack, staring at the kitten as if it were a four-footed time bomb, answered absently:

"Of course it was Manny. And I told you they went by here fast, I didn't notice his hair."

"Or his size?" persisted Blake. "Was he short or tall?"

"Manny's short, you know that," Jack sounded peevish.

But Blake held a new hope. Jack couldn't be sure; he admitted he had not had a good look at the prisoner. And, with this living evidence now purring as he stroked it, Blake was inclined to think that one of the agents might have been that captive. If so, he must have been a voluntary prisoner. Blake would never forget how easily Erskine had handled Beneirs. Unless the hiders were all shielded by Pranj's device. Blake frowned.

Had Jack not been helpless he would have gone after that party. He should know better than to interfere in the agents' business. On the other hand his intervention at the proper moment saved the game as it had at the Shelborne back at the beginning of this crazy adventure. But he dared not leave Jack.

The kitten climbed up Blake's arm and settled on his shoulder, rubbing its head against his chin and purring. He recalled the way Hoyt had trained it—the rapport the agent had established. Had Hoyt deliberately dispatched the little creature as a messenger? It was well-fed, sleek and unafraid. By those signs it had not been abandoned in the ruins.

"I must find out." Blake spoke more to himself than to Jack. But the boy raised himself on the pallet, his eyes shining.

"You're going after Manny!"

Blake evaded a direct answer. "I'll look around."

Before he left, he laid the rifle and the shotgun within Jack's reach, built up the fire and, across the doorway, erected a waist-high barricade. With the automatic and both knives as his own weapons, he was ready to start. But when he tried to leave the kitten with Jack, it uttered cat squeaks and clung to him with every claw so he had to keep it.

"Good luck!" Jack waved him off as Blake still hesitated.

"I'll be back soon . . ."

"Stay all day if it means getting Manny!" retorted the boy.

But when he went through the outer door Blake did not turn east in the direction the hiders and their prisoner had taken. Instead he searched the snow for the trail he wanted. Neat and straight, the line of tiny paw prints led up town. Half a block he traced them before they made a right turn between two houses. Crossing the backyard of one, they continued on over a rubble filled street, heading for a derelict gas station.

"How far did you come anyway?" Blake asked the bundle of fur whose bullet head protruded from the front of his jacket.

The kitten turned its round eyes up to his and squeaked politely. Blake gazed up and down the street. He had seen no tracks except those left by the dog pack and the kitten. The hiders had not come from this direction. And he dared not venture too far away from Jack.

Those paw marks in the snow beckoned him on, adding fuel to the hope he cherished. He need go no farther than just across the street, from there he could still hear any warning of an attack on the store.

The kitten's trail led to the smashed-in door of the service station. A tall figure stepped out to greet him as casually as if they had only parted five minutes before.

"Hello, Walker."

Hoyt! And behind him Kittson. Blake found himself clutching at an arm with his good hand.

"You've been through the wars," someone said.

"Come in, son, and tell us all about it," that was Kittson.

But Blake had control of himself once more. At least over his voice, though he couldn't keep his hands from shaking.

"There's a boy back there—badly hurt," he got out. "I can't leave him—"

Kittson's dark brows drew together in a frown. "Native?"

Blake nodded. Hoyt transferred the kitten to the front of his own jacket where it rode happily, showing the half-closed eyes of complete feline bliss.

"Is he able to walk?"

"No."

Kittson gave a resigned shrug. "We'll do what we can."

Blake felt a vast relief as the burden was lifted from his shoulders. Hoyt came out of the station, a pair of high-powered rifles on his arm, and both men started back to the store with Blake.

When he tried to give them an account of his past few days, Kittson stopped him. "Time enough for that later," he was told. "We'll see to the native first . . ."

That withdrawn concentration was on both their faces and Blake was silent. Were they working on Jack at a distance as Erskine had worked on Beneirs face to face? Because of his own shield he would never know.

They gave no attention to the three bodies in the outer room but went straight to where Jack lay quiet on the pallet. His eyes were open but he did not appear to see the agents and he showed no consciousness when Kittson knelt beside him. With quick, skilled hands the agent uncovered and examined the wound.

"Well?" Hoyt asked as Kittson rewound the bandage.

"He needs attention all right. We'll take him through to the base for treatment and return him with false memories, no trouble with his type of receptiveness."

Hoyt greeted that with a sigh of relief. "Suppose I take him through. That'll give Walker a chance to brief you. I can be back," he consulted his watch," in about an hour. Agreed?"

"You'll find us here."

As if Jack were a small child, Hoyt swept him up and strode easily out of the store.

"Hoyt will take him back to our own level. We have medical training which has outstripped that of most of the other worlds. The boy'll be cured and returned here with a false memory to cover the immediate past. He'll never know that he was out of his own world. Now—what happened to you?"

Blake spilled out the details, trying to sort out facts as if he were making a report to a superior officer. Kittson made no comments, but that aura of calm competence which surrounded the senior agent had its effect on Blake. He examined the dagger the other had taken from the dead hider, the one Blake was sure had come from the laboratory world.

"Ming Hawn," was his first remark. "So Ixanilia is one of his stops. That tower world, though, that's a totally new level—unknown on our recordings as far as I can tell. We'll investigate that later." He stuck the dagger point deep into a nearby piece of firewood. "You're infernally lucky, Walker. This may seem like a dangerous level, but I assure you that the comparative quiet of Ixanilia is far more deadly for the unwary invader. There is a hereditary nobility ruling there who have certain unpleasant pastimes—" the agent did not elaborate. "Pranj would be right at home in such a culture and we have suspected he'd head for there. But this importing of weapons . . . You say that that is a rumor among the natives here?"

"Yes, sir."

"Hmm. Well, Erskine has allowed himself to be captured by a group of hiders we believe to be Pranj's men. We would rather not contact the Sarge if we can help it. You seem to have done fairly well covering your own background with his people. In fact it's surprising—" but whatever Kittson had been about to say he did not voice. Instead he changed the subject. "Do you think you can find your way back to this cellar where the carrier left you?"

"I can try." But Blake was doubtful. "About all I know is the general direction."

"If they are taking Erskine there we shall not have to hunt." Blake guessed that Kittson must be in mental touch with the agent playing the prisoner's role.

"Are those hiders, the ones who took Erskine, wearing shields?"

Kittson smiled grimly. "No. We are hoping that that indicates Pranj's supply is exhausted."

Blake fed the fire and noticed the cans of food. He was suddenly aware of hunger. Now he pushed a pan of water closer to the flames and reached for a can opener and Kittson started to read labels.

"Rather a varied menu," murmured the agent.

"Mostly soups," Blake admitted. He measured chocolate powder into the bubbling water and opened another can. When he had the meal heating he sat back on his heels and asked a question of his own.

"*Is* your point of entry through that house on Patroon Place? And how did you get through after the explosion?"

"Yes to your first inquiry. The explosion, I believe, was a rude greeting arranged by our friends from Pranj's hideout. But chance brought your party there first and you must have triggered the bomb in some way so it did not catch us coming through as they had planned. The mop-up squad who collected Erskine will believe, when he gets through re-arranging their memories for them, that the rest of us were caught in the blast. That does smell good."

He accepted the mug of soup Blake handed him and sipped it slowly. Then he began questioning the other searchingly as to what he had learned from the Doctor and other members of Sarge's forces.

"I wish you could give the Sarge some help," Blake burst out, "some of the wonder drugs for Doc; they haven't developed them here. To clean up this city and rebuild. . . ."

But refusal was plain to read on Kittson's face.

"That basic rule of our Service is not to interfere. We're after Pranj because he *is* doing just that. If we did the same—even for good—how dare we arrest him?"

"But he wants to take over the world and run it," Blake protested. "You would only be helping a people who had it tough, giving them a better chance for the future."

"One can always discover good reasons for interference," Kittson replied. "We cannot and dare not meddle, either for good or evil. What can we tell about the influence even a good act may have on the future here? Suppose we give temporary relief to a small group of people? In that world that action will be like tossing a stone into a pool: spreading waves from it will circle out and out. We could save a single life and by doing so wreck thousands in years to come. We might prevent a war which would lead through exhaustion to eventual world peace on that level. It is not for us to judge or act. We swear to that when we enter the Service. We are observers only and our training fits us for that end. The other levels provide endless changes of action, but it is action in which we dare take very little part.

"Even such a mission as that we are now engaged upon, the eradication of a man who does strive to meddle in the other worlds, comes perilously close to the boundaries past which we dare not venture, not for our own good, but for the good of others. Yes, we could give the Sarge better weapons, the drugs, supplies, the assistance of a superior stable civilization. But by doing so we would defeat his cherished dream. What he builds slowly out of the wreckage through his own efforts and those of his followers will endure far longer than anything he could achieve with our aid. We must not lend crutches and so produce cripples. If you can accept that point of view—" Again Kittson broke off, almost as if he feared he had said too much. He swallowed the last of the soup. "Better put out the fire. It's time to go."

Blake obeyed, not surprised to have Hoyt enter a moment later. Their telepathic communication he now accepted as a matter of course. His only wish was that he could share it.

"Everything's under control," Hoyt announced. "The boy's going to be all right. Hakal will keep him dreaming until we are able to bring him back. Shall we move?"

Blake hesitated between rifle and shotgun. In the end, not knowing the worth of his marksmanship, he chose the latter.

"Contact?"

Hoyt nodded in answer to that clipped question from his superior. "They are keeping out of the park. Saxton's trailing and relaying. Stan's detected only one shield. The rest of the gang are malleable."

Blake offered information: "Jack says that everyone holes up at night. It's getting late."

They had come out into the street and Kittson glanced up at the clear blue of the winter sky. "Then we'd better make time while we've the light with us."

The agents, too, avoided the park, working their way downtown along a street a block away from its border. Birds called and wheeled above them, and once or twice they heard a muffled crash as wreckage thudded to the earth. Here and there, the snow was disturbed by the tracks of animals; the dog pack left their signature along with those of other furred dwellers in the ruins.

It was eerie, weird, to thread a path through all this when only days before he had walked through the same city—or its double—alive and vigorous with activity.

They had to make a wide detour about a bomb crater and then another where a pit which had once been part of the subway lay open to the sky. Kittson wheeled to the right and hastened his pace. The shadows of the buildings were as thick as the snowdrifts between them. Blake wondered how far they would go before darkness would make travel dangerous. He was startled when a blob of white detached itself from a nearby snowbank and came to join them.

Above the baggy, white covering, Saxton's face was as imperturbable as ever, though the rest of him bore little resemblance to the conventional businessman of Blake's level.

"Quite a gathering," he smiled at Blake. "We are heading into a meeting of some kind."

Kittson grunted and Hoyt asked eagerly: "They are getting ready to start something?"

"Not only they," Saxton brushed snow from his white covering. "I'd say that there is a small but lively war shaping up. Our gang was joined about fifteen minutes ago by a second party with another prisoner and they're headed straight for that group of ruins to the east. But we're not the only ones trailing them. I've counted at least three other scouting parties."

"That must be the Sarge!" broke in Blake. "I heard that he was going to have a big scale operation against the hiders."

"Complications," observed Hoyt.

Kittson made no comment but headed on, down what had once been an alley kept free of debris by some freak of fate. At its end was a barrier fronting on the wide boulevard rimming the parkway. Once they reached that the agents made no attempt to go on; in fact, Kittson dragged Blake down into the shadows.

The late afternoon sun glinted on metal moving among the winter-stripped brush on the other side of the wide street. A party of Sarge's men on the prowl?

"Ten," Hoyt's lips shaped the word rather than spoke it aloud.

Kittson's gloved fingers played with a broken brick from the mass before him. Blake gained a fleeting impression that the senior agent was annoyed at this development.

"We must reach there first," Kittson said, getting to his feet.

They crawled, they climbed, and at times they ran across open spaces. But for the most part they kept under cover, always boring into the choked core of what had once been the central section of the city. The tall towers were now mostly gone, their debris filling whole streets to second story level. But there were ways to be found through the stone jungle and the agents unerringly sped along these.

Blake noted that no matter how obstructions made them turn and retreat, they always eventually came back to a course which centered on a shattered tower suggesting in its outline the Medieval—a church. He wondered at this choice of landmark, but the others were certain of it.

Winter twilight was closing in as they paused in a cave which had been the display window of a large department store. Blake sniffed. There was a faint taint in the air, an unclean odor he could not identify. His three companions had frozen into the strange "listening" attitude, intent upon a telepathic search of the neighborhood.

"It is the church," that was Saxton. "They've posted sentries." His whisper was swallowed up in the emptiness of the ruins.

Blake heard nothing at all. If there were others moving nearbythey were so skillful in that progress that a non-psi could not locate them.

"Take care of those two—the ones in the north!" Kittson ordered. "Pick their minds first though!"

"Yes," Hoyt answered. "And I'll take the tangle-head three streets over."

Saxton pulled up the hood of his white robe. Against a snow patch he became invisible. "One Eye's mine." He made his bid mildly.

Kittson gave no verbal assent, but both men vanished in the dusk as if sucked away by the rising wind. The senior agent stood still, "listening." Blake was chilled through. The patched and wadded garments supplied by the park dwellers did not keep out this wind. He held first one hand and then the other to his mouth, blowing on stiff fingers which the mittens did not keep warm.

At last Kittson moved. He did not speak, but a jerk of his hand brought Blake after him. They crept along the edge of a building, keeping to the shadows wherever possible. Then the agent paused before a round mound of debris, molded by years of storms into a hillock of respectable size. This had to be climbed worm-fashion, wriggling their bodies from one projection to the next until they were able to lie at its summit and gain a view of the surrounding territory.

By some odd freak, a single building stood in the center of a flattened and devastated area. The Gothic outlines were unmistakable—this had been a church of cathedral size. And now its dark sides were glittering with gems of light where shreds of its stained glass windows were illuminated from within.

As the two watchers settled themselves for a cold vigil on the top of the mound, they saw a group of men emerge from the ruins on the other side and walk, with the confidence of those safe in home territory, across to the door of the church. Blake asked a question:

"Is this Pranj's headquarters? It's not where the carrier landed."

"It's a headquarters of some kind." Kittson pulled out field glasses and focussed them on the church door.

CHAPTER SIXTEEN

THE SNOW storms of the past days had left a wide carpet of white around the church to throw into sharp relief all parties crossing the expanse. It would be difficult, if not impossible, to make a surprise attack over that.

Kittson used the glasses on the doorway with concentration, but Blake shivered in the cold and wished they had chosen some less exposed spot from which to spy on the meeting place. He gave a start as a white figure detached from the ground and oozed up to join them. But Kittson did not turn his head.

"We'll have to move quickly." Some trace of preciseness still clung to Saxton's voice. "The group from the park are infiltrating the whole district. We could take over one or two squads, but it would require a parapsy-chologist to hold them all."

Kittson answered that with an impatient exclamation in a tongue Blake did not understand, though the profane meaning was easy to deduce.

"You located Stan?" he asked a moment later.

"Within six blocks," that was Hoyt. "What's going on down there?"

"Some sort of a conclave—they haven't started business yet."

"Maybe we have come at just the right time," Saxton suggested. "Could he have gathered them here to pass out arms?"

"Your guess is as good as mine. From what I've picked up so far, none of them know why they've been called in. Rumor has it that there is a big deal on." Kittson restored his glasses to their case.

"Our cue to go around and collect the star performer before he appears?" asked Saxton and then his voice was drowned out.

What Blake heard had at first no meaning, and then one so horrifying that·his mind refused to accept the explanation. The howling of the tower hags had been terrifying in its alien bestiality—the scream which carried from the church was even worse, for it could only have been born out of a human throat in the highest extremity of agony.

"Erskine!" He was on his knees, the shotgun in his cold-numbed hands. Then a steel grip dragged him down again.

At a second shriek, Blake tried to tear loose. They could not just stay there—listen to that—and know that their own friend was. . . .

"Not Erskine," the words reached through the red fog in his head. "That's some native they've amusing them-selves with." Kittson's voice was ice, hinting at depths of controlled passion beyond Blake's comprehension.

"We must—!" But in spite of his struggles, the other pinned him flat on the mound.

"We do nothing." Kittson was curt. "We'd be dead before we covered two feet of that stretch out there. The door sentries are shielded."

"Mark!"

But Kittson's head had turned even before that warning from Saxton. He was "listening," and then his breath hissed between his teeth.

"Good enough," he half whispered, "they'll mop up."

"*If* we can keep Pranj away!"

Kittson laughed, a humorless bark with the menace of a wolf's snarl. "Let the Sarge's men have a free chance to use that little surprise they're dragging in from the south, eh? Right you are, Jason. We'll attend to Pranj. He isn't down there, so we'll keep him from arriving."

Blake glanced from one man to the other. The dark was not yet so complete that he could not see their faces; there was the same emotion mirrored on their very dissimilar visages. They were hunters watching a dangerous beast stalk straight down a path leading to a trap. And now he was able to hear noises in the night. The scrape of an incautious boot, a smothered cough.

"What—?" he whispered.

It was Saxton, not Kittson who took time to explain: "The men from the park are moving in to attack. We disposed of the sentries for our own purpose and they have been able to get through the gaps undetected. They have a field piece with them and are manhandling it into position where they can knock the church to rubble. This is shaping up into a battle. They have the enemy cornered and will try to finish them off in one operation."

"Your doing?" Blake thought he understood.

He heard Saxton's chuckle, as warmly human as Kittsons mirth was not.

"After a fashion. We dare not really interfere, you know; but we introduced a few ideas into their heads so they believe the thoughts their own. If we can keep Pranj from getting control of the hiders long enough for the engagement to begin, we may drive him from this level and leave the natives to work out their own destiny."

Blake could hear, other movements in the dark, or thought he heard them. But he longed for the others' power to follow the unseen forces mentally.

"Time to go," Kittson announced. "You between us, Walker. Hook onto Saxton's belt and let him guide you."

They crept, they hurried, they hid, breathless, to let bodies of men pass them in the dark. The agents used all their powers to keep their small party from being discovered by the army gathering for the attack—all the while working their way from the vicinity of the church. Saxton knew the trail and they slipped from one dark pool of shadow to the next, avoiding the open and the wide patches of snow against which all but their guide would be visible.

Blake was not prepared for the sudden halt and bumped into Saxton as the three agents drew together.

"A sonic barrier!" That was Kittson.

"It went on full force ten minutes ago," Hoyt answered. "Pranj is in there. He's made at least three trips with cargo, according to Erskine's report, before we were cut off. They're holding Stan for Pranj to finish off later."

"We should have been prepared for this." Kittson's voice was self-accusing.

"Even if we had believed he could get a sonic through," Saxton pointed out, "what could we have done in the way of a counter move? There is nothing to break that kind of a barrier."

If there was discouragement in Saxton's voice, Kittson was not yet defeated.

"I wonder." He turned to Hoyt. "Where is the barrier?"

"End of this street."

Kittson spoke to Blake. "See if you can go to the end of the street and cross the space there. If you can, report back at once."

Not understanding, Blake obeyed orders. As far as he could see there was no barrier of any kind before him. The piles of rubble were no higher, no more forbidding than many they had already crossed that evening, and the night was quiet.

He stepped out onto the cracked and buckled pavement of the intersecting street. For an instant there was a shrill scream in his head, a noise which was also pain. But at his next quick stride that vanished, and he walked without hesitation to the other side, stood there for a moment, and came back to the three waiting for him a few feet from the point where the noise had struck him.

As he came up Kittson spoke to the others. "There's your answer. I didn't think Pranj would have it on the lower range. He couldn't if he wants to keep contact with the hiders."

"And he does that," Hoyt replied. "Erskine reports cases of weapons coming through and there are five Ixanilians there: three nobles and two red-cloaks."

"What do you want me to do?" asked Blake.

"Pranj has set up a sonic barrier no telepath can cross. Did you have any trouble?" Kittson wanted to know.

"Just a noise; it hurt my head."

"He'd feel something," Saxton cut in. "He's enough psi to be troubled by it."

"But he *can* cross it." Kittson returned impatiently to the most important point. "Somebody has to turn off that sonic and we can't get in there until it's done."

Blake was tired; his mind as well as his body ached with that tiredness. He had no desire to walk into the range of Pranj's power. And yet Kittson expected him to do that, as though he were another of the agents.

"Your shield," Kittson was continuing, "the one you used when he tried to get at you before. Can you use it again? Think of yourself as a frightened fugitive lost in an alien world. He knows you were marooned here; he may well expect you to turn up."

"Expect that I'd be hanging around in hopes of finding the carrier again?"

"That's it!" Hoyt supplied the enthusiasm Blake could not match.

"All right," he agreed wearily. "What does a sonic look like and how do I shut it off?"

Saxton provided the description. "It will be a black metal box about a foot square. There is a small crystal bulb protruding from the lid. Your easiest move will be to smash that. The minute you do it we can follow you in."

Hoyt unzipped the front of his jacket and brought out the kitten. "Pranj has a horror of cats; it amounts to a mania. The kitten will do as it has been trained. You may not go armed, but Missus will help."

Blake laid aside the the shotgun, the knives and the automatic, to put the kitten inside his jacket. Feeling remarkably naked, he started out along the way Hoyt pointed. He was across the barrier once more when, ahead, a faint green radiance and a distant hum proved that the carrier was in use not too far away.

He wrenched his mind from that thought; instead he concentrated with all his strength upon being lost, frightened, and alone—very much alone, striving to build up a picture of the past few days which would satisfy Pranj if only for an important moment or two, long enough for him to bring the agents to the scene.

Blake rounded a pile of rubbish and saw before him the half-hole which led to the cellar from which he had made his entrance into this world. Light streamed from the opening and he could hear the murmur of voices. He

173

drew a deep breath. Then he staggered, testing out how much he could waver without losing his balance.

Hunger, cold, loneliness, fear: he attempted to marshal all those sensations, think only of them, feel only them, as he stumbled toward the hole from which spread that alien, blue light.

The Ixanilians were not sensitive and not one of them was prepared for the arrival of that ragged figure which half-fell across the threshold. Blake blinked at light from portable lamps, dazzled until he was able to sort out the men staring at him in amazement. There were the brown skinned, arrogant noblemen he had last seen talking with Pranj in the laboratory building and two of their red-cloaked servants. And, his arms lashed to one of the pillars, Erskine stood, blood trickling from a battered mouth, his face black with bruises.

One of the red-cloaks caught Blake's wrists, forcing his arms behind his back in a practiced motion. The nobles conferred and their guttural speech was unenlighting to their new prisoner. Blake tried a trick Dan Walker had taught him long ago, stiffening his wrists as the red-cloak tied them. He was almost certain that with a little effort he could work free from those bonds. A contemptuous shove sent him not only halfway across the cellar, but to his knees, facing Erskine. One of the red-cloaks lounged nearby, but he gave neither prisoner strict attention. It was plain that the Ixanilians did not fear trouble from either captive.

Blake looked up at Erskine. Those pale eyes caught his and held for an instant, and then swept in a compelling message over his shoulder. Blake allowed himself to collapse. The red-cloak stepped forward, stared down into his face, and favored him with a kick in the ribs, which the captive greeted with a yelp of pain. But Blake gained what he wanted. At the edge of the rubble, which had concealed the arrival point of the carrier, flanked by a pile of boxes which the other red-cloak was methodically opening, was just such a machine as Saxton had described.

How he was going to get to it undetected was the problem Blake must now solve. The kitten moved against his chest; he felt the needle points of its tiny claws sink into his skin through his clothing.

The Ixanilian servant took guns from the boxes, odd looking stubby weapons which were the counterpart of the flame thrower he had seen. Armed with those, the hiders could make a clean sweep of the settlement in the park.

Blake tested the strength of the cords about his wrists, turning and pulling, feeling them yield just as Dan had promised. The kitten was growing restless and he was afraid that one of the others would see its movements under his jacket.

His captors talked among themselves. One of the nobles passed long, dark cigarettes to his friends and the acrid smoke puffed across the low-ceilinged space. But beneath their assumption of ease they were tense, wary, they did not relish this period of waiting.

Blake fought to relax. His warning stabbed knife-wise into his brain. Pranj must be on the way!

Green light behind the rubble . . . the hum. . . . The two red-cloaks jumped into action as the green vanished. Blake took advantage of their preoccupation to wrest his hands free. Then, his slim body encased in the clothing of an Ixanilian noble, Pranj came out into the cleared portion of the cellar.

The mask he had sworn as Lefty Conners was gone. Now he was the man whose image the agents had shown Blake so long ago. Power, self-confidence, radiated from him. He was smiling faintly, as if amused at playing at some task beneath his powers.

A word from the Ixanilians drew his attention to Blake.

On cat feet he came to stand over the prostrate American. Blake winced physically as well as mentally as the other's mind dart-struck. But he had had time to prepare: Alone—afraid—hungry—alone. . . .

He shut off all thought and tried only to feel. Fear—fear of this man, of the 'Lefty' who had changed—fear—alone.

Pranj laughed. Had Blake heard only that laughter, he might have believed it harmless mirth. But it did not match the cruel smile which was a matter of eyes rather than lips.

"Right back into the net."

Had he heard those words spoken aloud? Cold—hungry—fear— Feel: don't think, just feel. . . .

"Time for you later."

As Pranj turned away, Blake made his supreme effort and choked down a tiny spark of triumph. His hands were free. Now he must have a chance to use them—just one chance!

The excited voices of the Ixanilians were not high enough to cover the noise the red-cloaks made dragging more cases from behind the rubble. Pranj had transported a very full load.

But the interruption Blake had been praying for came almost on cue. A distant boom—dull, ominous, sounded. Those in the cellar were struck silent. Blake's hands flew to his breast and jerked open his jacket as guards and nobles clustered about the door peering out into the night. The Sarge's men must be firing on the church.

A second shot roared across the ruins, re-echoing until it sounded like ten. Blake, one hand grasping the struggling kitten, drew his feet under him, ready to spring for the sonic.

jumped to the left.

Pranj whirled. And in that same instant Blake exploded. He released the kitten before the outlaw and

There was a scream, but Blake had only eyes for the sonic. Though he stumbled, he flung out one arm and his fingers rapped its edge. The blow, slight as it was, jarred the machine back against the pile of half-open gun boxes and one of the weapons crashed down upon it. Blake tried to reach it, then a stab of torturing pain cut across the small of his back and he fell into blackness.

Battering waves of sound sorted themselves into a blaring pattern. Blake was conscious of cries, of a series of shouts. Some one stumbled and fell over his burned body, bringing a moan from him. And then the one who so held him captive writhed and screamed through a stench of burning cloth and flesh.

Blake lay still, aware that a battle was raging across the cellar. He dared not move; the least change of position added to his pain. But he tried to turn his head to see. Within the limited range of his vision lay one of the Ixanilian nobles and a second had crumpled in the door hole. Hoyt leaped that body.

So he had been successful. The gun falling on the sonic must have shattered the crystal!

The dull boom of the distant field gun was broken by the spiteful crackle of rifle fire. Blake wished he could ooze into the stone floor under him. But the dead weight across his body held him and he could not struggle for freedom.

Pranj backed into his view. He held one hand stiffly before him, and on its palm rested a bright blue ovoid. His lips were drawn back in a snarl of maniacal rage. The contorted face was no longer that of a sane man. The outlaw was doubly dangerous.

He supported the hand carrying the ovoid with his other, as if what he held was so precious or dangerous that it must not be shaken. A quiet had fallen on the cellar. It might be that those still alive were as concerned with the safety of that blue sphere as was he who bore it.

Pranj backed toward the carrier. Hoyt moved as slowly after him and then came Kittson. They had guns in their hands, but the muzzles pointed to the floor.

The outlaw laughed crazily. Then he tossed the ovoid into the air and leaped for the carrier. Hoyt sprang after him with the cry of a hunting feline about to kill. But Kittson remained where he was, his eyes focused on the blue sphere. It flashed toward him and then halted in mid-air as if enclosed by an invisible net. There was a runnel of sweat down the cheek turned toward Blake, but the agent continued to stare fixedly at the blue ball. He might be holding it suspended there by the power of his will alone.

Green glow and hum of the carrier in action did not disturb his stance. Erskine lurched into view, backing toward the door. With one hand he nursed a singed and spitting kitten. Then the weight across Blake was shifted and hands caught in his arm pits, bringing a choked cry of pain out of him as they dragged him up. Saxton hauled him to the door where Erskine, spent as he was, helped to pull him through. The Ixanilians sprawled motionless. Kittson still stood before the ovoid.

"I'm taking over," that was Saxton. "Now!"

Kittson leaped back as the ovoid wavered, dropped an inch floorward and then held steady once more. He picked up Blake, as if the American were no more of a burden than Jack, and went into the outer air in two great strides. Erskine waited them there and now Saxton came too, backing up the slope, his gaze still fixed on a point in the cellar.

With Blake, Kittson went flat behind a neighboring wall and Erskine joined them. As Saxton tumbled in beside the other three, the world came apart with a terrific burst of light and sound.

CHAPTER SEVENTEEN

THE DISTANCE booming of the field piece was regular, broken now and then by the crackle of small arms. Blake lay face down on an unstable support which swung and tilted under him. He did not try to understand what he heard or note his surroundings, being content to await what would happen next.

"*That has the sound of a full size war.*" The words were spoken above him.

"*It should keep their attention safely fixed there—for a while at least,*" was the answering comment.

"*The D-bomb must have sealed off this entrance for him.*"

"*We hope!*" There was a note of distrust in that. "*The sooner we can get to Ixanilia the better.*

Blake lapsed into a semi-conscious state. From time to time he roused enough to catch a glimpse of a light held on the path ahead, guiding those who carried him on the improvised stretcher. They were making better time through the maze of ruins than he would have believed possible. Yet the gray tight of dawn touched them before they reached their goal. When the stretcher was set down and his bearers moved away, Blake struggled up.

"With us again?" That was Erskine somewhere out of his line of vision.

"Where are we? What happened?" he asked the two questions foremost in his mind and Erskine answered the last one first.

"Pranj blew up his own station. We're now going after him."

Blake caught his breath at the stab of pain between his shoulders, felt when he moved, bracing himself on his hands, waiting for the walls about him to stop that sickening whirl. Though above was only open sky with a powdery snow drifting down, before him was a square cube of dull metal as large as a small room. And, even as he managed to fight off his faintness and center his attention on it, an opening appeared in its side to allow Kittson out. There was an air of impatience about the senior agent.

"Any message from Hoyt?" inquired Erskine.

"He's in Ixanilia."

"Time—"

Kittson nodded. "Yes, it's a matter of time now. If Hoyt weren't with him, it would be worse. Well, we have no choice but to follow."

Then he stepped over to Blake as though the American were some necessary piece of luggage not to be abandoned, rather than a person. He held out his hand but Blake had already wavered to his feet. When Erskine went through the door in the cube, Blake, supported against his will by Kittson, made the same journey. Once inside the structure, he discovered that it bore little likeness to Pranj's carrier. Here was a control board, cushioned seats, lockers for supplies.

Blake dropped into the nearest of the seats, hunching forward so that his back would not touch its surface. The hum was familiar, but here was no green radiance. Kittson took his place before the controls watching a dial with frowning intentness.

Erskine, his battered face still bloodstained, sprawled in another seat as though he did not care where they were now bound. But Saxton was alert, eager, nursing on his knee a weapon like the Ixanilian flame guns.

"Landings clear all the way?" he asked.

"Should be," Kittson made an absent reply. "Aloon

tested them on a trial run along these levels before we went on this case."

"It would be just our luck," Erskine threw in tartly, "if the Ixanilian one wasn't. I'd rather not materialize in the middle of a block of concrete. And it's half-past five in the morning; you may not have more than a half hour to get around without observation."

Although Blake could not see beyond the walls of the cube, he experienced once more that weird sensation of not being one with stable time or space. And he knew that they must be voyaging across the levels. Kittson pressed a button and the sensation subsided. They were fixed in time once more.

"We're in the clear," the senior agent announced. He picked up the twin to Saxton's flame gun before he opened the door of the cube.

"Warehouse," he informed the others. Saxton was ready to march. But Erskine pulled himself together more slowly.

Kittson came back to Blake. For a long moment he studied the American. Blake made an effort to straighten his hunched back, to give back that stare with authority. Then Kittson helped him out of his seat, transferring him without much volition on Blake's part to a place before the controls. Having settled the younger man there, the agent took from his pocket a small tube and shook out a capsule.

"Hold that under your tongue," he ordered. "Let it dissolve slowly."

Blake mouthed the capsule. But Kittson was not yet done with him. He caught up Blake's right hand and rested it on the control panel just below a button which gleamed with an inner spot of fire.

"If you get the order," he said emphatically, "you push that. Understand?"

Blake, his lips closed on the capsule, expended a small

fraction of strength on a nod and Kittson appeared satisfied. The three left and Blake was alone.

Strangely enough, as the long minutes passed, his head grew clearer, the pain in his back fading as he shifted position. He tried to recall all that had happened, but most of his memories of the night remained a jumble. Meanwhile he was tired of sitting there, watching the button, waiting. He was tired, hungry. He wanted nothing more than just to be allowed to sleep . . . sleep. . .

The cube rocked under him. Blake clutched at the chair with one hand and dug the fingers of the other into the board. Earthquake! The force of the upset could come from nothing less than an earthquake! Had he by some terrible mistake pressed the button and sent the cube traveling? No, his fingers were still a good three inches from it.

A clatter made him look around. Erskine half-fell through the door, and behind him burst Saxton, stopping to aid the slighter man as he came, hurling him at one of the chairs. He was gasping for breath as he spoke to Blake.

"Be ready!"

But their impetuous entrance was warning enough. Blake's finger was on the button as Kittson came in more soberly and jerked the door to. He gave the awaited order. "All right. Let's go!"

Again the hum, the whirl, the faint nausea.

"Two sealed," Erskine had recovered his breath. "Number three, now?"

"We've got him really on the run," Saxton agreed.

"You mean Hoyt has," was Erskine's reply. And there was a hint of worry in his voice.

Feeling more normal with every passing moment, Blake wanted to ask a few questions, but a glance told him that all three of the agents were now in their trance of speechless communication. Were they maintaining some thread of contact with Hoyt? Where were they bound now? To his own level?

Blake did not notice that they had reached their destination until Kittson stood up; then he was able to walk without assistance, after the others, into a very normal basement. The senior agent was consulting his watch.

"Eight-twenty. The Crystal Bird is closed. But there's that shop Lake rents out across the square."

Erskine leaned wearily against the wall. "He thinks it's all legitimate. Pranj had him under control, but good."

Kittson spoke to Blake. "When they picked you up, did they take you to a dress shop on the other side of the square."

Blake blinked. His adventure with the Scappa mob was so far in the past that he had to make an effort to recall details.

"I think so. But I was taken in there in a box of some kind. I couldn't swear to it."

"Those shops don't usually open until ten." Kittson looked at his watch again and then went on, the others trailing after him.

They came out of the cellar to the upper floor of the house on Patroon Place. The kitchen was empty and there was no sign of either cook or maid. The whole dwelling had the peculiar silence of a deserted house. At the windows, the shades were drawn, making the interior dusky, as the agents did not bother to switch on lights.

Boxes stood about as if the inhabitants were packing to leave. They edged among them into a room on the main hall near the front. Erskine snapped on electricity both there and in a small bathroom beyond. Catching sight of his own battered face in the mirror, he whistled.

"Butcher's meat," he muttered and began to strip, having put the now sleeping kitten down on a cushioned chair.

Kittson set a first aid box on a table top while Saxton

with surprisingly gentle touch helped Blake out of his clothes. Then he was pushed face down on the couch while the senior agent worked on his back. The comfort that the capsule had given him held and he scarcely felt their ministrations. Finally, with a thick padding strapped over the burn, he was left to rest.

"He couldn't have caught more than the edge of the beam," Erskine observed.

"Luckily. He'll do now until Klaven can see him," Kittson answered.

"Klaven?" Erskine sounded surprised.

"Can you suggest any other solution?" demanded the senior agent impatiently. And to that there was no reply.

"Breakfast." Saxton came back with a loaded tray.

Blake sat up. Much of his fatigue had vanished and he was more hungry now than tired. The food was strange; he guessed it consisted of rations from their home level. But the coffee was of his own world and he sipped the scalding stuff gratefully.

Refreshed he dressed in clothes Kittson provided: slacks and flannel shirt, with a heavy jacket loose enough not to fret his back. Erskine's delicate features were slightly more normal, though one eye was puffed shut and his lips badly swollen.

They ate swiftly and Kittson kept consulting his watch. Before they had quite swallowed the last bites, he was on his feet, leading the way to the garage.

He backed out a station wagon and they got in. They must be about to invade Pranj's base here, Blake decided for himself. The other three were all armed. But he had had no warning from his private source. Had the drug they had given him nullified that?

Kittson turned the car in the park and Blake wondered, for a bemused moment, if they were to overtake the Sarge's forces. It was difficult to drive along this road and remember that he was not in the other world—that there were two such stretches of artificial woodland.

The square which housed both the Crystal Bird and the dress shop was quiet in the early morning. One or two pedestrians were at the bus stop but there were no signs of life at either night club or shop. It was before the latter that Kittson pulled to the curb.

"All clear," Erskine reported aloud. "No one inside."

The senior agent went up the short flight of stairs to the main entrance. He cupped his palm over the lock for a second and then confidently opened the coor. A long hall running clear to the back of the house faced them. Paying no attention to the rooms on either side, they went down this to the back stairs, descending to what had once been the kitchen and service quarters. In turn, they discovered and used the steps to a second cellar, Saxton playing a flashlight along the floor, centering it at last on the well-opening in the floor.

Kittson stooped and passed his hand slowly around the rim of its cover before he gave it a sharp tug. One by one they dropped to the passage below. The way was roughly walled with brick and it ran straight ahead. They were perhaps two-thirds of the way toward their goal when Blake knew that his warning had not been nullified. He reached out to Erskine's arm.

"Pranj must be ahead."

None of them answered him, nor did they slacken pace. But, as they turned an angle in the passage, there was light ahead and Blake recognized the opening into the place where Pranj based his carrier.

"Two—shielded—coming—" Erskine warned.

Kittson strode into the carrier room and Saxton was at his heels. Blake hesitated. He alone carried no gun. Erskine was beyond, leaning against the wall with flame gun ready. Blake could see no way of playing sentry himself and stepped back to follow the others.

There was the level carrier. On it crouched Pranj, his lips shrunken against his teeth, a reddish spark in his eyes. Across his knee he balanced one of the flame guns, pointed at Hoyt. The red-haired agent's face was drawn and haggard. He had the look of a man close to the end of endurance. But his compelling gaze never left the outlaw.

Blake began to understand. The psi strength of the one held the other in invisible bonds. As long as either stood firm his opponent could not move. And neither of those silent, motionless figures paid any heed to the new arrivals.

What followed was a battle, the wildest, most improbable engagement one could conceive. No nightmare had prepared Blake for its moves. The agents did not try to overpower Pranj physically; they did not even advance to the carrier. But Blake was sensitive to the unleasing of vast forces.

Once, the gun was sucked out of Saxton's hands, whirled about in the air until it faced its owner, only to crash to the floor a second later. But Saxton made no move to pick it up again. A ball of orange-red light materialized in the center of the room, skimmed at Kittson's head, only to explode in a fountain of sparks which winked out. The light in the room dimmed, was almost extinguished, and then flared up again.

Then a creature crawled from beneath the carrier, a foul mixture of lizard and snake, talons on its feet, a forked tongue playing from fanged jaws. As it advanced, it grew more solid, more menacing. At last that flickering tongue scraped Hoyt's boot. But he gave it no heed. Then it sprang at him with a hissing scream, and was gone!

Blake shrank back against the wall. He was sure that they were illusions, weird weapons. But what purpose did they serve? Unless they were intended to distract the fighters.

Pranj still squatted on the raft, grinning his rat's snarl. He was not defeated; he was still able to hold at bay the agents. The final attack came from the passage. A shot, and then another—a scream. None of the three agents within moved.

Erskine! Had Erskine been——?

But whatever had happened out there meant something to the outlaw. He hurled himself at the doorway, at the same time shouting:

"In here, Scappa!"

But his lunge brought him up flat against some invisible barrier, against which he crashed with force enough to send him to the floor. The agents, snapping out of their trances, went to work swiftly. Hoyt jerked Pranj's hands behind him, fettering them with a hoop of metal Kittson had ready. Then the senior agent pulled over the prisoner's head a hood of silvery fabric.

Erskine loomed in the doorway. "Finished?"

"How many out there?" Kittson countered.

"Three. I think we have all those wearing shields."

"If we haven't we can mop up later," his commanding officer decided. "Once Pranj is back in Vroom they can send over a secondary squad."

Saxton slipped the carrying strap of his flame gun over his shoulder. With Hoyt, he carried the limp body of the outlaw over to the carrier. When the three of them were aboard, the older man gave a casual wave of his hand and took the control. The green mist shimmered and machine and men disappeared from view.

Erskine stretched. "Ready to go?"

Kittson nodded. They went out into the passage where the contorted bodies of three men lay. The two agents did not look at Pranj's dead henchmen any more than they had regarded the dead Ixanilian nobles. Kittson faced the door of the carrier station. He raised his hand and traced the edge of the steel portal which closed it from the passage. It fused tight, sealing the door so that Blake doubted if it ever could be forced open again.

They went back to the basement of the shop. And again Kittson sealed the well-entrance for all time. There were footsteps above, now, and the faint murmur of voices, but neither of the agents appeared uneasy. The fatigue Blake had felt earlier was closing in on him again and he dragged behind as they went up to the next floor.

A woman walked along the hall which led to the street door. But she gazed straight through the three of them, turning into a side room with no sign of alarm. They found the station wagon still outside, and got in.

"A clean 'solution satisfactory'," was Erskine's comment.

"Not quite," corrected his commander.

Blake leaned forward, his elbows on his knees, his chin supported by his cupped hands. He was sleepy, his eyelids heavy as lead. From the moment Pranj and his captors had vanished this lassitude had spread, not only through his body, but through his mind. Now he was interested in nothing but rest.

But when they returned to Patroon Place, he was jarred out of a doze and for the first time wondered what was going to happen to him now. On his fingers he counted off the days of the week. Only last Monday this adventure had begun; how far had he traveled since then? And now he was somehow sure that he would never return to the life he had had before he opened that hotel room door.

Once inside the house again, Kittson went directly to the cellar, his companions following him. It was not until they reached the level traveling device that the senior agent spoke to Blake:

"We can't leave you here."

He did not try to answer that.

"We can handle an open mind like Jack's. He'll be

returned to his own world remembering that you died in the explosion of the house. But that barrier of yours prevents us doing the same for you. And, with the information you have, we just can't leave you here. So," he hesitated, and for the first time since Blake had known him, appeared somewhat ill at ease, "so we have to break the first rule of the Service and take you along."

He waited as if expecting a hot protest. But between fatigue and the odd feeling that now this decision was the only one, Blake said nothing. They entered the cube; the door closed upon the world Blake knew. But he did not turn his head for a last look at it.

EPILOGUE

The Inspector gave his full attention to the information on the desk-reading plate. By rights, the file was closed. Only plain curiosity had made him trigger it this morning. He had a weakness for wanting to know the ends of stories.

Case 4678—when the 'Solution Satisfactory' had come through for that, he had wanted to learn the rest. And at the document he was now reading, he shaped a soundless whistle. It *was* a unique case after all! They had better watch that it didn't set a regrettable precedent.

". . . as the Council has been advised—reports of progress nine through twelve, filed by this group— we had no choice but to bring this individual from World E641 to Vroom. Report of Senior Parapsychologist Avan To Kimal (attached) agrees that subject possesses, along with power of precognition, a natural mind barrier to the 10th strength, a force hitherto undiscovered. There is also reason to suspect that subject may be from unexplored level EX508, which was destroyed in a chain-reaction explosion some twenty years ago. Circumstances of subject's introduction in E641 suspicious and EX508 was on the verge of discovering level travel for themselves when last disastrous war broke out. S. P. Kimal now investigating this.

However, being unable to leave him in E641 with false memories, we transported him to Vroom. The subject, though young is discreet, perserving our secret as well as any recruit. He is responsible for the discovery of level Neo 14 as yet unexplored. In addition he displays the ability to adapt and other useful qualities.

It is the considered opinion of this group that he is agent material, though not of our time or race. We unite in recommending him for further training and enrollment."

Quite a departure. The Inspector made a mental note—Blake Walker. It might be interesting to watch for that name on the rolls from now on.

He pressed a button and the plate cleared. 'Solution Satisfactory,' that was the way the Service liked them. The more such files they could present to the Council, the better. He yawned and prepared to close the office. Blake Walker— watch for that name in, say, three, four years from now. . . .

The Space Adventure Novels of Andre Norton is a special publication of The Gregg Press Science Fiction Series, edited by David G. Hartwell and L. W. Currey. The aim of the Series is to make available in quality library-bound hardcover editions those works of science fiction and fantasy that have proven to be of lasting interest and merit. The Series has already published more than 90 titles, most of them for the first time in American hardcover editions.

Gregg editions are not simply hardcover reprints. They all contain significant new material, such as critical introductions, charts, maps and other illustrations. For the serious SF reader Gregg offers the best editions of the best in science fiction. If you would like more information about the Series or a complete list of published titles, please inquire at your library or write to Gregg Press, 70 Lincoln Street, Boston, Massachusetts 02111

If you have enjoyed this book by Andre Norton, you may also be interested in **The Witch World Novels of Andre Norton**, a series of books set in an alternate universe where magic and science collide and fantastic adventures await readers of all ages. This Gregg set brings together for the first time in hardcover the following titles:

Witch World	*Warlock of the Witch World*
Web of the Witch World	*Sorceress of the Witch World*
Three Against the Witch World	*Year of the Unicorn*

Spell of the Witch World

Witch World includes a new introduction on the Witch World series by Sandra Miesel, together with a chart of all of the Witch World novels and stories, and all seven volumes feature new endleaf maps of the Witch World by Barbi Johnson.